KEY TO THE CITY

ʒɐ
of t'
anɗ
or
tʰ
sɪ

0(

K;

MATT WHYMAN

SIMON AND SCHUSTER

SIMON AND SCHUSTER
First published in Great Britain in 2005 by Simon and Schuster UK Ltd
a Viacom company

1 3 5 7 9 10 8 6 4 2

Simon & Schuster UK Ltd
Africa House
64–78 Kingsway
London WC2B 6AH

A CIP catalogue record for this book is available from the British Library

ISBN 0 689 87264 X

Typeset by Rowland Phototypesetting Ltd
Bury St Edmunds, Suffolk
Printed and bound in Great Britain by
Cox & Wyman Ltd, Reading, Berks

www.simonsays.co.uk

This book is dedicated to Grace

1

WHAT A WORLD!

Let's drop through winter clouds one night in the Year of the Snake, until London takes shape on the ground. From here, it's just a million points of light like the stars above. The River Thames divides the city. She may look like a glistening black serpent, but appearances can be deceptive at this hour. Pleasure cruisers are moored along the banks, while tourists from every country on this earth are tucked up in hotels for miles both north and south.

Sail in closer and the streets emerge, with terraced rows and high-rise blocks providing order to the tangle. Monuments and landmarks are bathed in floodlight – from Buckingham Palace to Nelson's Column – and form a pattern of their own. The London Eye may not turn until day cracks over the eastern skyline, but the big wheel makes the British capital look like an urban fairground.

Here, in these upper reaches, the chill is enough to freeze the blood. So, despite the attractions and distractions, it's time to plunge on towards a quarter at the heart of this metropolis. Within it lies a warren of side streets marked out from the rest by strings of paper lanterns and blinking neon dragons. A low fog may have crept out from the river, but swoop in quickly and we'll catch up with a small boy, careering over the cobblestones.

For this is London's Chinatown, and the kid is running for his life.

His name is Yoshi. He's thirteen years old, oriental on one side or the other, and soon that's about all he'll be able to say about himself. This boy may have a bright future ahead of him, but his past is set to become a mystery.

Behind him, an unseen force is closing in swiftly. Yoshi sprints through the deserted market now, upturning pushcarts and poultry cages. *Must. Get. Away.* He urges himself between breaths. *Can't. Go. Back.* He dares to glance over his shoulder. There's nothing to see but a soupy fog, which quickly begins to stir and draw in on itself. The boy doesn't need to hang around to know what's about to push through it. He snaps his attention ahead once more, only to barrel right into a stack of empty packing boxes . . . *Ooomph!* The stack collapses around him, but he's up on his feet and into a side alley before the last box hits the ground.

Now what's this? His first impression is of a

2

cut-throat kind of cut-through, but at least from here Yoshi can catch his breath and let his eyes adjust. He presses against one wall, head up high as he gulps the air. Seconds later, a shadow stretches across the street he's just left behind. Struggling not to squeak, Yoshi turns to make his escape – and finds himself face to face with a very dead end.

On one side he makes out a laundry, shuttered for the night, and further up a backroom kitchen with bins outside too full for Yoshi to climb into and hide. The door to the kitchen is ajar, however. The boy creeps towards it, on tiptoes now. Hot steam billows through the gap, with a light shining brightly inside. There's a chef at work in there, but the chop knife in his hand persuades our boy not to trespass in a bid to save his own skin. Instead, he creeps on by with his breath well bated. There's nothing beyond but darkness, but at least he can be sure that he's hidden from sight. Until, that is, Yoshi takes one step too far into the gloom, and causes several pigeons to flock into the air.

"There you are, child!"

With his heart in his throat, Yoshi spins to see a figure take shape at the mouth of the alley: a bull of a man in a long white mink coat. Beneath his furrowed brow both eyes are tight on the boy. His nostrils flare, and he takes a slow step forward. Yoshi backs away. A cry dies in his throat as he

3

connects with the far wall, only to gasp when his heel finds a drop just in front. Crouching among weeds now, he uncovers a grille of some sort: old iron bars buckled apart at the centre. If he breathes in deeply, he thinks to himself, the gap might just be wide enough for someone his size to squeeze through. Lowering himself out of sight, the boy hears the man's idle chuckling turn into a mystified growl, followed by thunderous footfalls.

The space he's in down here feels no bigger than a coffin, and that's precisely what the poor boy believes it'll become when two baleful eyes appear above the bars.

"Show yourself, little worm! Let's make this easy for us both."

"Get away from me!" In desperation Yoshi wriggles from a meaty paw. The litter that has gathered down here is damp and stinky, but the boy is prepared to bury himself in it to avoid being hauled out. "Do you hear me?" he cries out again. *"You can go to hell!"*

"Come and finish the programme like a good boy!" this fearsome figure bellows. "Let's make this easy for us both."

"I'd sooner die than go back again!"

Yoshi twists and turns until his pursuer quits trying to grab him. Glancing up, the boy catches sight of him reaching inside his mink instead.

4

"So be it," the brute sighs, sounding genuinely sorry up there. "If *I* can't put the squeeze on you then maybe this can . . ." What he draws from his pocket strikes terror into the boy: a *snake*, tail-first, and a long one, too. Hand over hand he uncoils this scaly rope, until a diamond-shaped head clears his coat with a hiss, and a forked tongue flicks towards the boy. "It's a vintage year for you, my pretty. And Yoshi here would like to help you celebrate it!"

Panic-stricken, the boy tucks tightly into his pit. At the same time, he senses that the floor feels unsteady. It's a sheet of corrugated iron, he realises, which is sagging with his weight where it meets the wall. Yoshi barely has time to take in the points of light breaking out as the sheet dips further still. What he can't ignore is the sight of the snake coiling around the bars, slowly invading his hiding space. It hisses again, so close to his face now that it might be whispering to him. All Yoshi can do is shut his eyes, praying that the embrace he can expect from it will finish him off quickly.

"You have a key to this city," the man growls. "If I cannot unlock what is mine, then you must take it to your grave."

"*No!*"

"Hey, mister!" Another voice cuts in, causing the man in the mink to stand tall and spin around.

5

He still has the snake in his grip, however, and its eyes seem to pop out on stalks at this sudden exit from the pit.

"The restaurant is closed. What's your business outside my kitchen?"

The chef! thinks Yoshi, but there's nothing left in his lungs to cry out for help. He sees his pursuer slip him a murderous glance, and then turn to explain himself:

"I'm catching rats," he offers. "Slippery ones."

"With a snake?" says the chef, suspiciously.

"It's a new form of fishing," the brute replies, sounding less sure of himself now. "You just cast your snake into the drains and wait for a bite, so to speak. You should try it," he suggests, with yet another glance at the boy watching through the bars. "In fact, you should've seen the one that got away just now."

The chef considers his story silently for a beat, clearly not buying a word of it. "Mister," he says finally, "any rats around here get their tails chopped off by me. The same applies to snakes if I find them lurking outside my kitchen, and that means human snakes, too, if you get my drift. Now scram, before I call out the boys from my backroom. They don't like to be disturbed from their card games, especially by sneak thieves."

"I'm not here to rob you! This is urban angling."

"Sure it is. Now, I'm going to count to three, mister. What's it to be?"

The man in the mink considers things for a moment, and then sighs heavily. From the pit, Yoshi sees him drape the snake around his neck, and then loop it like a scarf to keep out the cold. "Maybe I'll wait on the street," he grumbles, before making his reluctant retreat. "My rat's going to have to make a break for it some time."

"You do that," the chef agrees, sounding more relaxed now. "And tell your robber friends that anyone caught around here after dark is likely to lose fingers!"

Yoshi doesn't breathe out until he's sure that his pursuer has left the alley. He draws the air in deeply, and then promptly holds it in his lungs when the chef appears above the buckled vent again. Yoshi can't understand a word he's muttering to himself, but the chop knife in his hand gives out an unmistakeable message. His apron is spattered with blood, as is the blade that he swipes through the shadows now. If this crazed-looking cook is hoping to connect with cornered vermin, he comes close to a big surprise. Finally, with what sounds to the boy like a curse, he gives up and returns to his kitchen.

It's over, thinks Yoshi to himself, still shaken to the core by what he's just been through. The man in the mink might be lurking at the alley mouth, but the boy knows he has the time and space now to find a way over the wall and up onto the safety of the rooftops. He reaches up to climb out of the pit, not knowing whether to whoop or weep at his lucky escape. Popping his head through the bars, he's delighted to find the coast is clear. He savours the cold night air, his first taste of freedom ... and promptly takes it down into the depths as the pit floor drops away.

2

WELCOME, YOSHI

Am I in the underworld? This is Yoshi's first thought when he comes to his senses. If he is, then it stinks to high heaven and has cooked him up an infernal headache. He wiggles his toes and fingers, slowly reconnecting with himself, and then braves opening his eyes. His vision swims. The light in here is an eerie red, but the roof through which he fell looks quite solid. A line of hinges suggests it might be some kind of trap door, like the sort of device employed by a stage magician to make an audience member vanish. The only thing missing is a mattress to cushion the fall. Instead, Yoshi's sprawled on top of bin bags reeking of rotten fish. Without them, he would've broken bones. Then again, a hard landing might have kept him out for the count a little longer. Given the dreadful stench, it almost seems preferable. Even smelling salts wouldn't have roused him *this* quickly, which might explain why he feels so fragile.

Wincing now, Yoshi lifts himself onto his elbows. He touches his head, just to check it isn't cracked like an eggshell, and looks around feeling dazed and very confused. Three walls are made from brick and crumbling mortar, but the one behind him is solid steel. In the centre is a hatch with a flywheel. Above it, on a bracket, he spies a closed-circuit camera with a light on top. The camera, poised like some river bird stalking its prey, is aimed directly at him. Slowly, Yoshi clambers to his feet. The camera lifts a notch accordingly. Testing it now, the boy steps to one side, and again the camera keeps him in the frame.

Yoshi pulls a face, daring the lens to do likewise. The camera simply swivels, as if taken aback by his behaviour, and then the red light on top turns to amber. Next, a rumbling sound builds behind the steel wall. Yoshi backs into the brickwork behind him, wishing his head would stop hammering so he can think clearly.

The noise grows louder still, then halts abruptly with a thump. With nowhere to run or hide, all Yoshi can do is watch as the flywheel begins to turn. The light switches to green, causing him to catch his breath. And, with a squeak from the poor boy as well as from the hinges, the hatch pops open.

"*Ahoy!*" comes a voice from inside, sounding polished and noble like an old-school swashbuckler.

The light from within is so strong that Yoshi is forced to shield his eyes. Next a silhouette forms out of the glare, dipping through the hatch to join him in the cellar. Under the green bulb, it's clear that this apparition is human and no older than Yoshi. If his entrance had startled Yoshi then his outfit leaves him speechless. The breeches and bandanna certainly make the boy look like some kind of pirate. The roller blades, however, suggest something altogether more theatrical.

"The name's Billy," he says, looking down his nose at Yoshi. "Billy No-Beard, on account of the fact that I can't grow one yet. I keep trying," he points out, and strokes his top lip, "but savages like you think it's clever to call me Billy Bum-Fluff."

"I see," says Yoshi, and rubs his eyes just to check he isn't still out for the count. "I'll call you whatever you like if you can tell me what I'm doing here."

"I recommend a rest," says Billy next. "I've just watched you flee across half of London."

"You have?" Yoshi frowns, unsure what to make of all this. He can dimly recall racing through the night, and some drama in an alley, but anything before that is lost in the mist of his mind. Nervously, he runs a palm over his head. There's a bump back there so big it could slow traffic.

"You're pretty nimble for a landlubber, but you could've given that big oaf the slip much earlier.

11

Whenever you're in a tight spot, it's always worth looking down to find a way out. What did he want with you, anyway?"

Yoshi opens his mouth to explain everything, and then freezes. He looks mystified, at himself mostly. "I don't know," he says finally. "I can't remember."

"So what's your name?"

Again, the boy pauses, searching his memory for something. *Anything.* "I . . . I forget."

"What's with the dog tags?" Billy rolls forward, and draws his visitor's attention to the chain around his neck. Inspecting the nickel plates, Billy pinches them both between his fingers as if estimating their value. "Says here you're Yoshi. *Yoshi 5.*"

"It does?" Yoshi is as surprised to discover he's wearing two tags as he is to learn he has a number as well as a name. He finds the plates with his fingers, and looks down his nose to examine them. Several digits are engraved on the second plate, he discovers: an eleven and a twenty-three.

"What's that all about then, Yoshi 5?"

"Search me." The boy spreads his palms wide. "I'm totally lost."

"Then allow me to conduct a short tour." With a swaggering spin, Billy No-Beard returns to the open hatch. "Don't be scared. You're safe as houses inside this tub."

Cautiously, Yoshi steps over the threshold and

into the blinding light. With his head still throbbing, it actually hurts to look around, but it seems he's in a corridor lined with plumbing pipes and pressure gauges, air vents and bare wires. The metal decking clanks with every step, while his roller-blading guide rumbles on noisily ahead.

"Mind your head," warns Billy as he sweeps left and hops through an open hatchway, though there's no danger of Yoshi connecting with the pipes.

Even if he did, the boy thinks to himself, it couldn't make his headache much worse. "Where am I?" he asks.

Billy is waiting for him, one boot tipped onto the toe brake. "This is the Galley, where I do the cooking."

Yoshi scans the surfaces and sink. "What about washing up?" he asks, unable to ignore the piles of dirty pots, dishes and half-finished noodle cartons.

"It's a problem," agrees Billy, only to move on before Yoshi can press him to explain what a place like this is doing way below street level. "Over there is the canteen, and through these doors here is the central ladder. It'll take you to the showers, which it seems you badly need," he adds, wrinkling his nose. "The sleeping quarters are on the same floor, while the lower level houses the Engine Room. It's totally self-powered and blast-proof, with no reason to shut down for centuries. I believe she's been producing light, power and hot water for over twenty years now. I'd show you round myself but I've only just laced on my wheels for the day. Unless you want to give me a piggyback down two flights and back again, you'll just have to take my word for it: this old tub is entirely shipshape."

"Are we in a submarine?"

"Don't be silly. We're smack bang under the heart of London. Ask me something sensible. You do have questions, don't you?"

"Erm, lots actually," says Yoshi, still amazed that such a space could even exist. He looks up, hoping for an explanation, but his guide has gone again.

"Keep up, Yoshi 5! As you can see I am *way* behind on domestic duties!"

The boy pops his head back into the central corridor, sees Billy turning circles at the far end before vanishing into another room. With a sigh Yoshi heads in his direction, trying hard to ignore the nagging sense that he is not alone down here with his guide. It's the way the hairs on his neck have started to needle that makes him think he's being watched. Nursing the back of his head still, he wonders when his memory will stop swimming with so many question marks.

"Will you please slow down and tell me what's

going on!" he demands, finally catching up with his skate-happy guide. In response Billy turns to face him, and then simply steps to one side. What Yoshi sees still doesn't explain why he's here, but it's enough to stop him in his tracks.

"Oh boy," he declares. "It's mission control."

The room is filled with monitors and radars, arranged in rows and facing a big screen on the far wall. There are complicated-looking control panels at each post. Some are blinking wildly, and walkie-talkie chatter can be heard from a speaker somewhere.

"This is the Bridge," says Billy with a note of pride. "The command post on our humble bucket."

The equipment looks very old indeed, but everything appears to be working fine. Yoshi scans all the monitors, in awe at the sheer scale of the space. Some screens switch between shots of fog-bound street corners and junctions, plazas and station entrances, while others are frozen on what looks like the same video game.

"Do you play?" asks Billy, stepping up to one monitor now, and offering him the handset. "We've got beat-'em-ups, drive-'em-ups, shoot-'em-ups, boot-'em-ups, sing-'em-ups and stealth-'em-ups. You'll find every kind of *up* down here, in fact. But I warn you, I'm hot when I'm on a roll. I'm Lord of the Light Gun Game and the Virtual Skate Czar, natch." He studies his nails, buffs them on his shirt. "What do you say? Let me challenge you to a round of *High Seas 4: Storm Warning*."

"I don't want to play games!" insists Yoshi, his patience thinning. "Just tell me how I can get out."

Billy No-Beard seems surprised at his response. He tips his head to one side, as if perhaps that might help him understand Yoshi better. "Just a quick round?" he suggests, lifting an eyebrow hopefully.

"No!"

"I'll let you go first."

"This is ridiculous," Yoshi declares, and winces as his skull tells him to keep a lid on the volume. He touches one temple, his memory still blank as the moment he came round on a bed of bin bags. "Right now my whole life feels like it's been turned upside down."

"Then welcome to our world, Yoshi 5."

The boy looks up smartly, if only to confirm that what's just been said hasn't come from Billy.

"There's someone behind me," he suggests, appealing to his guide to help him out, "isn't there?"

With his lips flattened white, Billy simply motions with his finger for Yoshi to turn around. It's been a night of surprises for the boy, but finding several dozen urchins standing in a crescent at his heels is enough to make him jump. What's more, in the middle stands a striking old man who must've appeared in a puff of smoke. He's wearing a long and colourful patchwork coat, and his hair and beard are as wild as they are white. With his broad nose and brow, Yoshi is reminded of some wise and stately lion. Judging by the wrinkles that bracket his china blue eyes, he could be one hundred years old or more.

"You've come a long way," the man says with a smile. "We're delighted you could drop in!"

3
OUR KIND OF MAGIC

"Who on earth *are* you?" asks Yoshi, his surprise overshadowing all fear.

The man steps forward and offers his hand. He's beaming at the boy now, pleased with what he sees. "My name is Julius. Julius Grimaldi."

"Pleased to meet you, sir," says Yoshi, remembering his manners, if nothing else.

"Oh, no need to be so formal! Just call me Julius, and we shall call you Yoshi. We'll even do away with that number of yours to help you feel at home. If you're as lost as you look, consider us your new family."

"Thank you," says Yoshi, taken aback by such hospitality, "but I really should be returning to wherever it is I've come from."

The old man seems genuinely surprised. "You're free to leave, as is everyone, but it can be a jungle up there. We find that kids who stumble upon us tend to be in need of some shelter for a while. You might as well stick around until your head feels a bit better. Make yourself comfortable, dear boy. If there's anything you need, I'm sure we can conjure it up."

"Are you a wizard?" blurts Yoshi, and immediately wishes that he hadn't when the boys and girls behind him giggle and titter among themselves. None of them look like apprentices, he realises belatedly, even though the man is dressed like some master magician. Apart from Billy No-Beard, most are sporting worn-out skate gear, hippy rags, chopped up punk haircuts and army surplus accessories. It's a strange combination, almost tribal, but somehow he feels safe in their company.

"Don't believe everything you read in books," says Julius, chuckling to himself. "If I could cast a spell do you think I'd be stuck here? Those bars you squeezed through are wide enough for skinny-ribbed kids maybe, but it would take a miracle for a man of my size to climb out of there."

"You make it sound like you're a prisoner," says Yoshi.

Julius smiles at the suggestion. "I have my own ways of escaping," is all he adds. "Besides, dear boy, it doesn't matter *where* you're holed up. The mind is always free to roam."

At this, one of the kids in the background rolls his eyes and circles a finger around his temple. Yoshi tries hard not to giggle, but it's enough for the old man to surface from his thoughts. He looks a little bashful, as if perhaps he knows he's alone with this outlook on life, and then recovers to step back with a flourish.

"By way of introduction," he announces, beaming down at the rag-tag pack, "why don't you all show our guest your kind of magic?"

Even before he has stepped aside, a plume of emerald-green flame shoots up from the open doorway. Yoshi jumps with a start and shields his face. When he dares to look again, a thick mist has enveloped the room – and yet none of the kids have scattered.

In fact, they all appear to be floating some centimetres above the ground.

"Hey!" he cries, looking up and around for an explanation. "How are they doing that?"

Julius Grimaldi is standing away from them now, with Billy still sulking at his side. "My crew like to make an impression," says Julius proudly. As he speaks, the hovering band of kids with him spreads out, until Yoshi is entirely surrounded. He turns in amazement, giddy with shock, stunned all the more when they begin to switch fireballs over his head. He wheels around, barely able to take it all in, even when Julius commands them to stop.

"The boy's been through enough for one night," he tells them. "Give him some space now."

With a gentle patter of feet, this circle of angels comes back to earth. Yoshi continues to turn, staring in amazement at one kid after another. It really is too much for his head to take in, from the bump in the cellar to the spectacle he's just witnessed before his very own eyes.

"I think I should lie down," he says weakly, and begins to spin out completely. This time, however, someone is there to catch him when he falls.

During the 1980s, when today's adults were school-kids, the world lived under threat of total war. Nuclear bombs were the weapon of choice, designed to wipe out millions with a single blast. Thankfully, it never happened. Even so, government leaders and army generals in every country made preparations to protect themselves and survive – just in case one side or the other tried to turn the earth into a smouldering lump of space rock. First of all, they made a big show of their weaponry, like *that* would calm the situation. Then they built themselves bunkers – underground command posts where they could take cover if it all kicked off. Mercifully, everyone woke up to the fact it would be a conflict nobody could win, and concentrated instead on sorry-looking hairstyles and get-rich quick schemes.

As for the bunkers, many were simply boarded up and forgotten over time. Such was the pace of development on the surface that these reinforced hideaways became lost to the world above: just another leftover from a bygone age. But like any fossil, buried in seams underground, there will always be *someone* with an interest in uncovering the past.

For an urban explorer by the name of Julius Grimaldi, the discovery of one such space below London must've been like striking gold.

To the untrained eye, the vent Julius had uncovered at the dead end of the alley seemed unremarkable. What persuaded him to investigate was the military blueprint in his possession, and a desperate need to keep it out of the wrong hands. He may have been younger at the time, but nowhere near as slight as Billy or that strange troupe in there with him. For any grown up, the squeeze between the bars would've been an almighty challenge. Nobody willingly forced themselves through such a narrow space that they suffered cracked ribs in the process, so Julius must've known there was no going back. Then again, like all the ragamuffins and runaways who would come and go while they could, the safety on offer was worth more to him than anything in the world.

*

Right now, many years after Julius first claimed this space for London's lost children, this very same bunker is home to a new arrival. There he is in the Sick Bay on the second floor, down opposite the sleeping quarters. With a flutter, his eyes open. He blinks, and slowly focuses on the presence watching over him.

"Yoshi's with us once more," says Billy No-Beard. "Let's hope some sleep has persuaded him to find his feet on the dance mat. I had to take my blades off so I could carry him down the ladder, so a quick game of *Shake It All Over* is the *least* he can do for me now." Billy's comment is met with a sigh, followed by a playful cuff around the head. "That hurt!" he cries out, and glares across at a lad with spiked red hair and a nose ring.

Vaguely, Yoshi recognises him from the welcoming party that had gone on to take his breath away. He strains to lift his head from the pillow, thinking perhaps he might glimpse feathery wings between his shoulder blades.

"Play nice, Mikhail," says Billy, repositioning his bandanna now. "It's the first rule of gaming. Respect your opponent, win or lose."

"Billy, go tell Julius that Yoshi has come round, and then fix up a bowl of won ton soup." Every word that leaves Mikhail's mouth sounds like it has been clipped and put through a roller. He has an ice-cold accent that leaves Yoshi thinking of old spy movies. "Our comrade here needs nourishing food to get strong again. Not stupid games."

"*Stupid?*" Billy covers his mouth, shocked to the core, it seems. "How dare you talk about gaming like that? You're only bitter because you were begging for mercy last time we played *Fencing Master Mayhem.*"

"Just find old Julius," says Mikhail, more forcefully this time. "There is a time for games, and a time for you to vanish." He jabs a thumb at the door. "Why don't you practise your disappearing act?"

"OK, OK, I'm going. There's no need to be so rude!" Flushing angrily, Billy No-Beard breaks for the central stairwell. "Mikhail is from Siberia," he says to Yoshi on the way out, like that will explain everything – and not just his thick Russian accent. "It's a cruel and savage place, by all accounts."

Billy turns and slams the hatch behind him. Mikhail shrugs, but Yoshi has just one question on his mind.

"How did you guys do that thing?" he asks.

Mikhail wrinkles his nose, making the ring through it twinkle under the lights. "What thing is that?" he asks, clearly playing with Yoshi. "You mean levitating?"

"What else! It isn't every day I see a whole bunch of people hover in the air."

"Don't believe everything you see, Yoshi."

"But you lifted off the ground and span around until I saw stars!"

"I'm sorry if we shocked you. Judging by the narrow escape you made last night, it's clear you'd been through a lot." Mikhail comes forward to inspect Yoshi's head. "That bump is a beauty."

Yoshi feels for the bruise and winces. "It's unlike me to take such a bad tumble," he says.

"Yeah? Why is that?"

Yoshi frowns, looking at a point between them. "Do you know what? I can't remember."

"Maybe you were just unlucky," Mikhail suggests. "Who was that guy chasing you, anyhow? The one with the big white fur coat and the pocketful of surprises?"

Yoshi stares at him blankly, then shakes his head.

"You really *have* lost all memory," sighs the Russian boy. "Julius has high hopes it'll all come back to you soon. He was the one who first spotted you on the screens, in fact. Making a dash from Piccadilly Circus. Personally, I didn't think you'd make it with that beast breathing down your neck. The way you escaped impressed us all. It proved you can survive by your wits. It means you'll fit in nicely, if you choose to stay."

Yoshi looks at the ceiling light, trying hard to tune back into whatever it is he left behind in the world above. "Maybe I should just report myself missing to the police," he suggests. "Someone must be wondering where I am."

"There's certainly one individual who'd be pleased to see you, but judging from last night I doubt he has your best interests at heart."

"But what about family? I must have one somewhere."

"In this city," says Mikhail with a sigh, "Missing Persons posters go up every day. Believe me, a lot of us like to keep one eye on them. It's our way of knowing if anyone is out there looking for us."

"Like parents?" asks Yoshi, perking up now.

Mikhail shrugs. "Mostly we're not wanted, but if your face does happen to show up you'll be the first to know. For the moment, though, you're safer down here with us."

"So who are you?" asks Yoshi, sitting up now. "More importantly," he mutters to himself, "who am I?"

Mikhail shrugs again, snaps his fingers and a deck of cards appear miraculously in his hand. "Let me read your mind," he says, grinning now. He fans the pack face out and lets Yoshi see them for himself. "Take a card," he offers. "Don't show me, but focus on it hard. Let me pick up on your thoughts. It might even tell us some surprises about you."

Yoshi frowns suspiciously, but does as he is told.

He selects the ace of clubs, but doesn't blink or betray any sign that Mikhail might detect.

"What now?" he asks.

"Return it to the pack. Anywhere you like." With the card handed back as requested, the Russian boy sets about cutting the deck at random. Finally, he spreads all fifty-two cards into a fan, studies them for a blink, and causes one to wiggle outwards. "The ace of clubs." He turns it to show the boy. "Is this the one you picked?"

Yoshi looks from Mikhail to the card and back to him again. "OK, so how did you do that?"

Mikhail pockets the deck. "First rule of street magic," he says. "Never pull the same trick twice. The first time, people want to be amazed. Second time, suspicion takes over. You need to leave them spellbound, not wise to your ways."

"Are you suggesting I'm supposed to learn this stuff?"

"Another good reason to stick around!" Mikhail pauses to help him off the bed and onto his feet. "Every kid who can fit through the bars goes out with the tricks of the trade. Old Julius doesn't have much time for our kind of magic. Even so, he knows it's a sure-fire way to earn some pennies from the tourist hotspots around town. He supplies the shelter. We bring in the food and the charts or whatever it is he requests."

27

"Has he really been down here for years?" Yoshi climbs from his sick bed, testing his balance before standing freely.

"Since before any of us can remember," says Mikhail. "He has probably done more to map the city under the surface than any other urban explorer."

Yoshi looks at him quizzically. "So he isn't trapped inside the bunker?"

"The military fitted bars above the entrance when they'd finished with it. With everyone out, I don't suppose they saw much point in sealing up the emergency exit." He jabs a thumb over his shoulder at a steel plate in the wall. "If the generals and their staff ever needed to make a hasty getaway, they'd simply climb into the chute behind there and slide their way to freedom. Julius has given up using it. The clamber back to the top makes his bones ache, but we use it to come and go."

"Where does it lead?" asks Yoshi.

"That's classified information," replies Mikhail playfully, and taps his nose to show how top secret it must be. "Let's just say there *might* be a military monorail that leads to an airport out of the city. If the general public knew about that, it wouldn't be a secret any more."

"There's no such thing," protests Yoshi. "Is there?"

"According to Julius, the line has collection points under the Houses of Parliament, government ministries and the Palace, in case the important people needed to get out of town in a hurry. But like so many levels under London, it's no longer in use. Nobody goes down there any more, apart from us."

"Isn't that trespassing?" suggests Yoshi.

"Who's going to catch us?" asks Mikhail. "As far as the military are concerned, the tunnels and this bunker are history. They've found other ways to blow their budgets on bigger, better toys. But for us, it's everything we need. So long as this hatch is sealed from the inside, nobody can get in. The only way in from street level is through the bars, and no adult can hope to squeeze between that gap. For kids like us that means a lot," he says to finish, "to some more than others."

"I think it must mean a great deal to you," says Yoshi, when the boy drops his gaze for a moment.

"All of us have run away from something," says Mikhail eventually, "just like you."

Yoshi nods, wishing he could make sense of his arrival. This time, an image flashes across his mind's eye: *a man in a white mink coat, searching the streets for something.*

What's weird is that it doesn't feel like a memory. Yoshi had torn through darkness and fog to escape this guy. And yet the impression he has now is so bright it flares just like the sunshine he can see on the brute's bald dome. It's like a clip of some sort that could be playing out right now, somewhere on the surface of the city.

Yoshi furrows his brow, concentrating harder, only for the picture to pop into little pieces as fast as it had formed. He shakes his head as if to clear it, finds his new friend once more, and puts the moment down to the big bump on his head.

"I know I arrived in a hurry," he says, nursing the bruise now. "I just wish my brain would stop playing tricks so I could remember what it is I'm running from."

"All in good time," the young Russian assures him. He chews on a thought for a moment, says finally, "Speaking of tricks, would you like me to show you how I guessed your card?"

"Yes, please!"

Mikhail produces the pack one more time, only for a siren to begin wailing through the bunker. He sighs and, with a flick of his wrist, makes the pack vanish from sight. "All hands on deck!" he yells over the din, and moves quickly for the door. "Little tricks like this are just the beginning, Yoshi. Here's your chance to see what we do best."

4

ACTION STATIONS!

Yoshi scrambles to keep up with his new friend with the flag-red hair. Other crew members rush ahead on the stairs, all of them flocking to the upper level. By the time he follows Mikhail to the Bridge, there's a kid in front of every computer screen. Billy rolls between each row. He's sporting a headset now. It has a little microphone on a bar in front of his mouth. He seems very pleased to be the one barking orders.

"Tangos on cam three, d'you copy? I say again, we have four tangos in total, approaching south from Covent Garden tube station."

"*Roger that,*" a voice crackles over the main intercom. "*What are they packing?*"

Billy glances at the nearest monitor. On the screen, an overhead camera appears to be tracking a family ambling through a crowded street.

"Tangos are wearing matching yellow windcheaters. Adult male has a video camera slung over left shoulder. Looks like adult female is wearing the bum bag. Proceed at will, copy?"

Yoshi struggles to take it all in. Both eyes bug out, while his jaw slowly loses the fight against gravity.

"In case the authorities happen to be listening in," whispers Mikhail, 'tangos' is our code for targets. Right now, the tangos are tourists. We've hit the jackpot if they turn out to be American. They always have deep pockets. Just like the Japanese and the Swedes."

"Please don't say they're about to be robbed," pleads Yoshi, watching the two children saunter along happily in front of their parents. They're clearly enjoying the atmosphere out there. Street entertainers compete for their attention – a juggler balances a chair by its leg on the tip of his nose, while buskers belt out classic songs on anything from banjos to bongos and even dustbin lids. The place is bustling, colourful, but relaxed. Almost *too* relaxed, thinks Yoshi fretfully.

"Just watch," suggests Mikhail.

The big screen at the front of the room fires up to reveal the family in close-up. On Billy's order, the camera pulls back. It brings some street punk into the frame – hands in pockets, whistling to himself – who tags behind the woman.

"Bravo Team Leader, you're clear to go on my

word." Billy glides by Yoshi now. "Your soup will have to wait, kiddo," he tells him, covering his mouthpiece for a moment. Yoshi is about to declare that it's too late – for this whole affair is leaving a bad taste in his mouth, but already Billy has swung back around to the big screen. "Go, go, *go!*" he yells by way of command. "This is not a drill!"

At once the street punk's hands dart forward. It's a blur on the monitor, but then he breaks away and it's clear to Yoshi that he's clutching a wedge of passports.

"*Bum bag located,*" the punk confirms over the intercom, picking through his find as he melts into the crowd. "*The goose just laid four fine, golden eggs.*"

"No!" yells Yoshi. "This is wrong!"

Nobody turns to face him except for Billy, who scowls over the monitors.

"There's more to this than meets the eye," Mikhail assures Yoshi. "There always is, with us."

On the screen, the street punk appears to have finished going through the passports. Yoshi watches him double back to rejoin the family, walking close behind the woman again. Another blur of hands, and when he breaks away this time, the passports have gone.

"*Eggs returned to the nest,*" he confirms over the intercom. "*Will regroup with Bravo Team immediately.*"

"Good work, Team Leader," says Billy. "Here's

hoping we can hatch the eggs without a hitch. Bravo Team, are you ready?"

"*Copy, Billy. We have a visual now. Tangos are on their way.*"

With a crackle of white noise, the main screen switches shots. This time, it focuses on a motley crew of kids hanging around bollards where the street meets a square. The pickpocket that Yoshi has just been watching walks into the frame. He joins the pack, who gather round for a brief moment and then break apart like someone has just dropped a bad smell. A second later, the family appear. They slow to a halt – confronted, it seems, by a question from one of the kids.

"What's going on?" asks Yoshi, upon which the kid draws a deck of cards from thin air, just as Mikhail had. He fans the deck effortlessly, and shows it to the family. They look hesitant, but this scamp has a winning grin. It's enough for the father to overcome his reluctance and pick a card. He shows it to his wife and children, all of them pulling faces like this will never work, and then returns it to the pack.

"The kid you're observing is one of our best. Not only has he bet that he can correctly guess the card, when he shows it to them it's going to have their names and birth dates miraculously scrawled across it."

"Maybe he could do the same for me," mutters Yoshi, sensing some kind of trick take shape. "I could certainly use the information."

"There's plenty of time for that." Mikhail touches a finger to his lips. "You're missing a master class here. You'll note he's involving the whole family in this trick. Working the crowd is far more effective than focusing on one person. It makes individuals less likely to question what they're seeing for fear of ridicule from the others. We like to call it our weapon of mass delusion."

Yoshi watches the street kid shuffle the pack, pinpoint a card as if following some higher instinct, and then face it to the family. This time, they respond as if he's just flashed them a glimpse of tomorrow's headlines. They turn to each other in amazement, their mouths forming perfect circles, while the kid stows the cards, dusts his hands and holds out his palm expectantly.

Yoshi only has to see the money cross this punk's palm to realise what he has just witnessed here, and can't help but be impressed.

"That was so cool," he says, watching the family move on with smiles painted wide across their faces. As soon as their backs are turned, the kid lifts his attention to the camera and gives the thumbs up. All around Yoshi, the boys and girls at their monitors begin to whoop, cheer and swap high-

35

fives. All except one eagle-eyed lad near the front, who stabs a button near his screen so his voice comes across the intercom.

"Cops on cam five, Bravo Team, approaching from the Strand. They'll want to know why you're not at school, my friends, so time to make yourselves scarce."

"Roger that. Returning to base."

Gradually, the jubilant buzz on the Bridge returns to a workmanlike drone. As the kids begin to move around, returning to posts and positions, Mikhail leads Yoshi to one side. "What you've just seen is street magic in action."

"I'm impressed," says Yoshi. "But it's hardly magic."

"That's because you saw how it was done. Through the eyes of that family, what happened defied all reason, but we know it's just a deception."

Yoshi can't help but look a little downcast. "Don't you feel guilty?"

Mikhail draws air between his teeth, thinking through the question. "It's tough to accept that what you see is just a trick," he says finally. "Everyone wants to believe that there is more to this life, after all. We're simply in the business of suggesting that dreams can come true."

"Well, if you put it like that," says Yoshi, though

it's clear to Mikhail that his new friend has some reservations.

"Before we showed up, those tourists were practically sleepwalking through their visit to London! We just gave them a little wake up call, and brightened up their stay. Even better, we got paid for it. So, everyone is happy."

"Hey," says Yoshi, enjoying the sales pitch now. "You've won *me* over."

"It's all about preparation," says Mikhail. "Thanks to this camera network we can carry out some of the greatest feats in the history of illusion. We have Billy to thank for that. He's the one who restored the feed from New Scotland Yard's traffic cams, and set up the firewall so our computer system is invisible to them. With an eye on every street in the West End and the surrounding area, we're talking big business. Sometimes we'll make a few pennies from an operation like that. Other times it can amount to a small fortune. It all depends on the trick and the tourist."

"And this is what you do, day in and day out?"

"Like I keep saying," grins Mikhail. "There's more to us than meets the eye."

Yoshi watches the crew settle down again, wondering if things can get any more crazy, only to attract the attention of the boy in charge of operations.

Billy No-Beard wheels across the floor, accepting instructions over the headset. "There's no space in here for observers," he breaks off to tell the boy. "Besides, Julius has just radioed in. He wants to see you in the Map Room."

"Where's that?" asks Yoshi.

"You want me to give you directions?" Billy smiles slyly. "To the *Map* Room?"

"I'll show you," says Mikhail, shaking his head now. "Did I tell you that our cabin boy is also the resident wise guy?"

"I'm an Executive Deck Hand," Billy says to correct Mikhail, clearly stung by his description.

"That's fine," says Yoshi, palms up, for the last thing he wants is a conflict. "Whatever you want me to call you is not a problem."

"And Number One Game Champ," adds Billy as they pass, as if anyone could've forgotten. "Whenever you're ready for a round, Yoshi, just say the word. I'm beginning to think you're a top player who's trying to fool me into thinking you've never picked up a joystick in your life."

"I've no idea *what* I am," says Yoshi with a shrug. "I just hope that if my memory comes back I'll like what I discover."

5

DEEPER DOWN

Mikhail reaches for the brass door knocker, and gives it a hefty whack. It seems odd to Yoshi for such an old-fashioned device to be fixed to a blast-proof steel door, but then nothing seems normal since he last saw daylight. In vain, the boy's been searching his mind for some clue that might tell him who he is. All he can be certain about is that life down here feels somehow more secure than the life he's left behind.

The door to the Map Room is half open, but the boys stay out on the deck plate, awaiting a response. When it arrives, the distant, mumbled *"Enter"* tells Yoshi that the man they've come to see must have his mind on other matters.

"This is where he does his thinking," whispers Mikhail. *"Shhh!"*

They've come down to the bunker's lowest level. It's really just a narrow, dimly-lit gantry that rings the Engine Room. If Yoshi turns around he can see it through the viewing glass: a hulking great core of riveted steelwork, pumps, flasks, switches and pressure gauges that seems to rise up from oblivion. Yoshi peers through the gaps in the deck plate. He can hear dripping far below, as if they're standing over some kind of chasm. It's almost a relief for him when they step over the threshold and into the Map Room, even if it does take them down a series of iron steps and onto cold flagstones.

"So glad you're with us again, Yoshi! I'll be with you in a moment."

With no sign of the old man, Yoshi looks up and around. The walls in here are towering, with bookshelves climbing high. There are ladders on rails to reach the upper shelves, all of which are crammed with tomes from every age. At the very top is a skylight. Every now and then, dark spots trail across, taking shape and then peeling off from above.

"You're looking at pedestrians," says Mikhail. "You must've walked over glass bricks in a pavement before?"

Yoshi focuses on the square of flat light, thinking hard. "Of course," he says. "I haven't forgotten what it looks like up there, but if you asked me to find my way home I wouldn't know where to begin." He finds the dog tags hanging from the chain around his neck, rubs one of the plates between his fingers.

"Eleven twenty-three," he says to himself. "These numbers must mean *something*.

"They're too long to be a house number," Mikhail points out, "and too short for a telephone number. You're not old enough to play the lottery, but it might be a pin number for an account containing a million pounds!"

"Do you think so?"

"I *wish* so, Yoshi, but who knows? It could be anything. If it's a code of some sort then Julius is the right man to crack it." Mikhail crosses the floor to a large circular table. A candelabra stands in the centre, with a ring of wicks burning brightly. Light flickers over the paperwork strewn around it, and a chess set with a game in progress. The candle-light makes the pawns appear to advance as the Russian boy pores over the set, studying the next move.

"Numbers are what makes his world go round," says Mikhail, drumming his fingers thoughtfully on the table. "Present him with a pattern, he'll unpick it."

"So where is he?"

Mikhail nods towards the far end of this cavernous room. It goes beyond the reach of the candlelight, but as his eyes adjust Yoshi spots a passage with a dim light of its own. The bare earth walls are shored with timber, but the boy can't help thinking he's in some kind of human badger's sett. Oil lamps hang from the joists, revealing a gallery of picture frames of different shapes and sizes. "When Julius filled the Map Room with his stuff, we had to dig him some more space. That's the advantage of underground living. If you need more room to breathe, simply grab a spade!"

Just then, a slanted shadow passes from the wall of the passage to the floor. The sound of someone muttering to himself grows with it, and then Julius Grimaldi appears around a corner. He seems puffed, like he's come a long way, and shuffles out clutching so many scrolls that the boys offer to help without being asked.

"No need. I can manage!" he insists, and promptly stumbles on the edge of a flagstone. The scrolls spill across the floor, one rolling to a stop at Yoshi's feet. The boy crouches to collect it, and rises to find this snowy-haired oddball looking sheepish but thankful.

"I'm not as sharp as I used to be," he admits, as the Russian boy retrieves the other stray scrolls and begins stacking them in his arms again. "If it wasn't for the likes of kind-hearted kids like Mikhail, I'd have starved to death down here. Either that or I'd have learned to enjoy the taste of stewed rat. Are you hungry, Yoshi? You must eat to get big and strong."

"Ah, I think I've just lost my appetite, actually."

"Yoshi was wondering if you could tell him what the numbers mean on that thing around his neck." Mikhail scoops up the final scroll as he says this. He turns to give it to Julius, who drops the lot for a second time.

"Good Lord," the old man whispers, his eyes wide in awe. He stares at the nickel plates for what seems like an age. "I had no idea you were wearing tags. You're lucky it's just your memory that's in a pickle, dear boy. I'm surprised your mind isn't messed up, too."

"Really?" Yoshi slides his gaze to Mikhail, who shrugs as if the old man's musings are beyond him. With a big sigh, he stoops to pick up the scrolls again. "All I remember is a chase, and a man in a white fur coat," continues Yoshi, "but nothing more."

Julius nods, as if the boy's arrival makes complete sense to him now. His focus on Yoshi sharpens so intently that Mikhail clearly thinks twice about trusting him again with the scrolls, because he dumps them on the table instead.

"If I'm right," says Julius eventually, "it's a blessing you don't remember anything more than that."

"But I want to know," insists Yoshi. "I *need* to know who I am, where I've come from, and how I can get home again."

"For the sake of your safety," insists Julius, "you really should accept our invitation to stay."

"I feel like you guys know more about me than I know about myself," says Yoshi, clearly frustrated. "Maybe I should stick around in case you can tell me what's going on."

Julius smiles kindly. "In time, it won't seem like such a puzzle. Right now, however, all I can say is that these numbers round your neck tell me everything and nothing."

"So is it a code for a bank vault?" asks Mikhail. He presses his hands together in prayer. "Please say we're millionaires."

"That's for us to discover," says Julius, and then flattens his lips behind his blizzard of a beard. "But if there's a fortune in store for Yoshi it isn't the kind you can spend. There are other kinds of riches in this world, you know?"

Mikhail looks like he's finding it hard to accept this. He draws breath to protest, only for the bunker air to be seized by the sound of the siren again. "Must be another operation," he yells over the din, backing towards the iron stairs. "If it involves making anything vanish then I should be out there leading the team. I do the best disappearing tricks in the West End. Let's go!"

"By the time I make it to the Bridge, it'll all be over," Julius chuckles and waves him away. "Leave the poor boy with me. He might enjoy a tour under the town."

Yoshi remembers the emergency exit that Mikhail had shown him. "Will we be going down the chute?" he asks, blocking his ears as the siren continues to wail.

"Goodness no! At my age, there are some things best left to the youngsters."

"So how do we get out of here?" asks the boy.

"The civilised way," says Julius, simply. "This bunker is designed to withstand a nuclear strike from the skies. The military didn't regard moles and worms as a major threat, so I had my crew here cut through into the sewer below."

Yoshi looks at Mikhail, mystified once more. "It can be kind of gross," the Russian boy tells him. "But as long as you don't hit high tide, it beats travelling by tube, bus or car. No crowds, traffic lights or fares to be paid, either."

"Indeed, it's the finest gateway into London," adds Julius. He pauses there, distracted for a moment by the blaring siren. "Mikhail, you had better get up to the Bridge. Billy is capable of running the show, but without you around to keep him in check there's bound to be a drama."

Mikhail turns for the stairs, pausing only to throw a brief farewell to Yoshi. "I'll catch up with you later," he promises. "Maybe then I can show you what's up our sleeves. It's about time you learned some proper tricks!"

"Sure thing," says Yoshi, wishing he could remember someone on the surface, if only so he could see the look on their face when he revealed what was down here. Then again, if he painted a picture of this madcap old man the chances are he'd be laughed at in disbelief. In his patchwork coat, Julius Grimaldi looked like some kind of Victorian explorer trapped in time. It's an impression the boy finds hard to shake as Julius searches the shadows between two bookcases, and returns with an ancient-looking telescope.

"Come with me, dear boy," says Julius, ushering him towards the passageway. "It's time we did some sightseeing."

6

TELL ME WHAT YOU SEE

It's hard to keep track of time when you're underground. Without a sun or moon to help anchor your place in the day, all you can do is go with the flow and prepare to be surprised when you surface.

For Yoshi, it's been one long string of shocks since we first fell upon him. Right now, he's in a dusty old wine cellar that opens up over his head into a towering stone shaft. A series of iron rungs lead all the way to the top. High up there, a creaking old man in a flowing patchwork coat has just lifted himself onto a ledge. He makes himself as comfortable as he can on this narrow perch, and then peers down into the lamplight at the boy's feet.

"Don't be scared, Yoshi. I've made the same climb every day for decades. It's perfectly safe."

"I'm not frightened," he calls up, and steps back to remind Julius what he has carted all the way here. "I'm just scared I'll smash your telescope."

"Have some faith in yourself, dear boy!" Julius

pauses there, and fishes out a pocket watch. "But we must act swiftly."

A brass cap covers the telescope lens, but Yoshi doubts that will help to protect it should he drop the thing ten metres. *Oh well*, he thinks, and lifts it over his shoulder, *Julius has got me here in one piece. He must know what he's doing.*

From the moment Yoshi had followed him out of the Map Room, Julius moved with a spring in his step. He appeared more upright and sparky, and not just because the boy had foolishly offered to carry the telescope. No, it was as if Yoshi's arrival in the bunker had given the old man some kind of purpose. At the time, Yoshi had wished he would slow down, and not just because the weight on his shoulder was making his arm ache. Mostly it was so he could check out the spectacular gallery of charts, sketches, blueprints and engineering diagrams that lined the passage walls. Every one was contained in an ornate frame, like some weird exhibition of a city picked apart to the bone.

"Is this London?" he had asked, hanging back for a better look.

"The city under the surface," Julius confirmed. "London underground is so much more than a rickety tube-train system and a clapped-out network of oversized Victorian plumbing. There are ancient burial chambers and catacombs down here, bank vaults, mine shafts, panic rooms and priest-holes. And the deeper you go, of course, the more history you uncover. The foundations themselves are centuries old, but the bedrock underneath has been around since the dawn of the earth."

"*Wow*. Even if I could be sure I've lived in London all my life, I doubt I've ever thought about it like that."

"For the people who live on street level, this subterranean world is out of sight and out of mind for good reason. What we don't know tends to scare us, after all. A place of urban myth and legend, perhaps, dug up for nighttime stories to keep little ones in bed."

"Like the myth about the giant alligator living in the sewers?" Yoshi had suggested, which amused Julius no end. "I may not be able to remember where I heard that story, but everyone knows it!"

"Do you mean the tale about the pet reptile that was flushed down the toilet when it grew too big to be kept in an apartment?"

"Uh huh."

"The one about how it grew to *massive* proportions on account of the fertiliser that runs off the fields around London and into the water system?"

"That's the one!"

"It's no myth," Julius had said, not smiling any

49

more, and promptly dismissed this detour in their conversation by steering him along the gallery. "Yoshi, I have made it my life's work to map the history and geography of London under the surface, but every new discovery presents another one just waiting to be explored."

"You must get around." Yoshi had cast an eye along the walls, trying hard not to think about Mikhail's mention of some short cut through the sewers.

"Quite so, dear boy. As in life, it's all about tracing the connections." Julius had pointed at a chart beside the boy. "You're looking at a cutaway view of the tube network, just to show how deep it goes. The one above it uncovers everything you wish you didn't know about the sewers, and that beauty opposite singles out the service tunnels. The Royal Mail have underground train tracks used exclusively to transport post from one sorting office to another, did you know that? Many of the tracks are in a state of disrepair, of course. They're pitch black and rat-infested, but that isn't a problem if you're well prepared for such a journey." At this, Julius had reached up to unhook an oil lamp from a roof joist. He held it high, looking set to turn and lead the way, and cast a light on some of the frames that had been in shadow.

"What about that one?" Yoshi had asked, his eye

drawn to a simple sketch of the city boundaries, with thick pencil lines scribbled inside.

"The lost rivers," said Julius with a sigh, clearly anxious to be moving on. "Tributaries from the Thames that have been buried or built upon over the centuries. There are said to be twelve in total, some still flowing happily deep under the streets, all shopping-trolley free as well. Indeed, I have stood upon the underground shores of the Fleet, Stamford Brook and the Falcon, and very pleasant they are too, but others remain a mystery to me. Now, please keep up, dear boy. We have some way to go."

Julius had swung around with the lamp, revealing a manhole cover in the floor of the passage behind him, but Yoshi remained genuinely entranced. For the next frame to capture his attention had shown a page ripped from an A–Z street map.

Yoshi had recognised it immediately: the centre of London Town.

Every street name seemed familiar, as if perhaps this was his home ground. And yet the closer the boy had studied the network of roads, terraces and squares, the more his memory refused to provide directions. It didn't help that someone had defaced the map with a black marker pen: drawing a jagged flower shape around the city's heart.

"What does this mean?" he had asked, inviting a frustrated sigh from up ahead.

Crouching to lift the manhole cover, with the lamplight burning beside him, Julius had turned and said simply: "Oh!"

"Well?" Immediately, Yoshi had sensed that this was more than just an act of graffiti.

"It's a seven-pointed star," Julius confessed after a moment, breathing out as if it was a relief to share the information. "Geometrically speaking, we refer to it as a septagram. In mystical circles, it's known as the Faerie Ring. The number seven is what makes it so special. It governs so much of our lives, from the days in the week to the colours in the rainbow, the number of oceans in this world and the continents, too. There are even seven pressure points on the human spine, and seven openings in the head," he had finished, whisking a finger from his eyes to his mouth and nose, and then back to the map on the wall. "Seven is everywhere, and is summed up as one by the Faerie Ring."

"So what's the meaning of it?" the boy had asked, studying the skewed shape. The star's diameter had spanned the city, reaching out at seven points to cross roads and public buildings, rundown estates, royal parks and palaces.

"Give it time, Yoshi, and this may become something you can answer for yourself."

"I wouldn't know where to begin."

"Then let's push on, Yoshi, for I intend to take you to the very place."

By the time the boy begins the climb up the column now, his eyes fixed on Julius at the top, he's ready to believe anything. The journey here has opened his eyes to many things. First Grimaldi had unlocked the manhole cover and dropped down with his lamp. Yoshi had followed with a prayer on his lips and his nose firmly pinched between his fingers. Mercifully, the sewer was dry underfoot, not to mention alligator-free. According to the old man, this one served as an emergency overflow. Some days, so he had warned along the route, there could be unfortunate moments when too many citizens flushed their lavatories and emptied their baths and sinks at the same time. Yoshi had hurried after the old man, anxious to be out of the pipe, and deeply relieved when Julius shone his lamp up at another manhole cover about a hundred metres along the way.

With a helping hand from the urban explorer, Yoshi had climbed out to find himself on the soot-covered ballast bed of an old tube track. His shoes are wet from where they had gone on to cross a deep-level viaduct, and his heart is still hammering since dipping under the nose of an old, war-time bomb. There it was, poking through the vaulted roof of a culvert, and still capable of exploding, according to the old man who had inched past it so carefully. It seemed incredible to Yoshi that so much of the capital could be hidden from the world above ground. Despite the dangers, it also seemed strangely thrilling.

Directly below Julius at last, Yoshi holds on tight to the last rung inside this strange column, and reminds himself not to look down.

"Now what?" he asks, scanning the cramped and gloomy space above the old man. He counts six sides at the summit, each sporting a circular stone plate.

Julius checks his pocket watch one more time. "If I'm right, we've made it with just minutes to spare." He winks at the boy next to him. "And if my clock is out then at least we've come to the right place to correct it."

"Huh?"

"You'll find out soon enough."

Yoshi watches as Julius spreads his gnarled fingertips over the plate in front of him and gives it a gentle push. With a click the plate swings outward, much to the boy's astonishment, before Julius moves on to the next one. Seconds later, moonlight is flooding in from six angles, as well as the hum of a city under the stars.

"Where are we?" asks Yoshi.

"About a mile north-east from the bunker, in a place called Seven Dials." Julius shifts around to let the boy see for himself. "These plates are clock faces. Sun dials, to be precise."

"But there are only six," says Yoshi curiously. "Where is the seventh dial?"

Julius chuckles, and offers his hand to help Yoshi up. "We're in it," he reveals. "This *is* the seventh dial. As the sun moves around the pillar, so too does the shadow."

"What happens at night?" the boy asks, amazed more than anything to find a whole day has passed since he first discovered this underground world.

"That's why we're here," says Julius. "Many of London's earliest architects were also great mystics. These founding fathers looked to the skies for inspiration, and designed buildings with the sun and the moon in mind. Some even used the inter-play between darkness and light to help us see things that would otherwise be invisible to the eye."

"Like the time," says Yoshi, struggling to keep up.

"The sundial is one small example," the old man concedes. "But just look around you now," he suggests, as if this will help Yoshi make sense of things. "Tell me what you see."

7

AS ABOVE, SO BELOW

It's a squash at the top of the pillar, providing just enough room for Julius and Yoshi to face out through the open sundials. Together, they peer over the moon-silvered rooftops like pirates in the crow's nest of a ship that's run aground. Seven narrow avenues surround the monument, all of which are flanked by tall, cramped buildings. The city is quiet at street level, which makes Yoshi think it must be late. A taxi circles the roundabout, and a drunk somewhere sings a gutter serenade.

"It looks so familiar," Yoshi breathes, scanning the pitched roofs, sundecks and balconies, "but different in every way."

"That's because you're looking at it from the inside out," says Julius. "Of course, it doesn't help that dropping in on us as you did appears to have reset your memory, but I'm confident we'll find out what makes you tick. Now study your surroundings. I want to know what goes through your mind."

Yoshi turns as best he can, taking in the gables, gargoyles and roof gardens that so often go unnoticed from below.

"It's a blank," he says sadly. "But what a view!"

"One of the finest," agrees Julius. "And for good reason."

Yoshi looks up at the old man beside him. Puffing hot breath into the air, Julius invites the boy to count the number of church steeples he can see on the skyline.

"Well," begins Yoshi. "I see one over there, another to the right, and over there is number three." He turns to peer through the open clock faces behind him. "Four, five and six." He comes around full circle. "And one more makes seven. That makes seven steeples, Julius! Some far away, some closer. So what?"

"Does the pattern seem familiar?"

Yoshi thinks about it, tries drawing it in the air with his finger.

"Imagine looking at it all from overhead."

Slowly, the boy seems to picture it. Counting out seven points now, he completes the star shape and looks at Julius.

"It's the pattern I saw on one of your maps," he

57

says, sounding very pleased with himself. "That's a clever discovery."

"All the churches you have counted were built by Nicholas Hawksmoor, following the Great Fire," says Julius. "Now *there* was a city architect with vision."

Yoshi studies the steeples once again, aware now that the seven streets spreading out from the monument further complicate the arrangement. Despite his loss of memory, Yoshi senses that he had always considered London to be a random tangle of roads and lanes and alleyways. But now it seems the city has been founded on a grand design, as if the landmarks were arranged to satisfy a certain order.

The question he goes on to ask Julius is why.

"If only I knew, dear boy," he says ruefully. "I consider myself a master archeoastronomer, but the more I discover about this city the more mysterious it becomes."

"Excuse me?" Yoshi pulls a face. "Archeo-*what*?"

"I apologise," says Julius sheepishly. "Perhaps it's easier to think of me as a psychogeographer."

"You're losing me," the boy tells him. "I may not recall anything about my school life, but I'm pretty sure we didn't sit down for lessons in psycho-whatchamacallit and astronoma-doodahs."

"*Archeoastronomy*," Julius repeats, stressing the

word this time, "and *psychogeography*. If they don't teach you these disciplines at school it's no wonder the youth of today have become a generation of slackers!"

"Give it to me in a nutshell, Julius. A sentence is about all my head can handle at the moment."

"Very well. I study the relationship between our urban landscape and the heavens above, and its impact on the human mind."

"Nope." Yoshi shakes his head. "I'm totally lost."

"Look up," Julius suggests. "What do you see?"

"Stars. A lot of stars."

"What shapes, Yoshi? Look at the brightest points of light."

"I see the Bear, the Plough and . . ." he tails off there, having spotted the very same pattern he has just traced out with his finger.

"You're looking at seven planets, Yoshi. It's an alignment that often comes around in the astral calendar to form—"

"– a Faerie Ring," the boy cuts in, his eyes wide with wonder. Now he can see it for himself, the star formation blinks and twinkles like a necklace of jewels. "I'd never have noticed it if you hadn't pointed it out. Now, it's the only thing I see."

"On Earth as it is in Heaven," says Julius under his breath. "As above, so below."

Yoshi turns his gaze on the man, finds him

looking out across the city skyline. "Excuse me?"

Julius smiles, seemingly pleased at the boy's keen interest. "That these buildings form geometric patterns is no accident, agreed?"

"If you say so."

"And as I told you on setting off, the seven points in the ring are rich in meaning."

"The same number as the days of the week and the colours in the rainbow," says Yoshi, stealing the words from the old man's mouth. "My life before I fell into your bunker might be blank, but I don't think I'll forget what's happened to me since. If you say seven is special, so be it."

Julius nods, without turning from his view of all the pitched roofs and chimneys. "Depending on your capacity to believe, Yoshi, the seven points in this ring are *very* special indeed. In sacred circles, they are said to represent the seven levels of psychic energy that govern our universe and beyond."

"Psychic energy," the boy echoes, only this one comes back at the old man with a strong note of disbelief and ridicule. "Are you trying to mess with my head?"

With one long finger, Julius taps at his temple. "Let's just say it's a form of energy up here, in the mind, and all around us. It's in the soil, the sky, and every last atom. If the lights went out in God's own house, he's put money in the psychic energy meter. Only select mortals are able to tap into it, of course, but for those who can it's a spectacular power source. Through time, the Faerie Ring has always been thought capable of hosting the highest form of psychic energy. In fact, some reckon the lines running between the seven points can be used as channels for forces of both darkness and light."

Yoshi's eyes shift from the stars to the steeples, and across to the old man beside him. If a panic alarm had been fitted up here, the boy would be reaching for it without hesitation. "I don't mean to be rude," he declares, "but that's the craziest thing I ever heard! Are you suggesting the city is ringed by some kind of magical boundary?"

"You could say that," he says. "But if you think I've lost the plot then we'll head back to the bunker and you can learn how to fool people with the *illusion* of magic. What I've brought you here to see is the real thing." Julius stops there for a second, as if perhaps he's said too much too soon.

"No, I'm listening," says Yoshi, thinking it would be a shame to return to the bunker now, having come this far.

Julius considers the boy for a moment. Finally, the tension eases from his face. "Yoshi, there is the kind of magic that you see on stage and on the street. It's a fine skill, and one that can earn a small fortune, but it's really just entertainment. A persuasive force, perhaps, but that is all."

"It impressed me," says Yoshi, reflecting on the card tricks he had seen earlier.

"Harnessing the force that concerns us here dates back to primitive man. I'm talking about *magick*. The rare ability to tap into psychic energy, and bend it to your will. It doesn't require wizards or broomsticks, potions or strange brews. If you're tuned in to this force, I guarantee you'll go far. My studies in psychogeography and archeoastronomy uncovered the existence of this ring around London, but it's vital that you come to it with an open mind."

"Well, I certainly have one of those," says Yoshi, and reaches for the back of his head. "There's plenty of space to fill since I've forgotten everything there is to know about myself!"

Julius chuckles, pleased and relieved by Yoshi's response. "Are you willing to learn?"

"Go ahead," the boy says. "Tell me how this ring thing works."

8

THE GREATEST TRICK

For the residents of London, there is only one ring around the city. It's an orbital motorway, used by commuters as a slingshot between home and work. Satellites just outside the earth's atmosphere can see this six-lane loop. At the end of the day, if you're stuck in a jam, you might be lucky enough to look up and spot one glinting in the twilight. This happens when the sun meets the horizon. Then, the last rays gleam from the mirrored wings and dishes of these high-flying eyes. They can light up like comets, sailing from one dusky horizon to the next, only to be lost when the stars come out in force. Sometimes, another spectacle can take shape in their place, though this one can be impossible to pinpoint amid the swirling soup of galaxies.

Unless, that is, you're lucky enough to be with someone who sees things on a different level than most folk.

From their vantage point inside the Seven Dials,

Julius considers the twinkling arrangement now. He dwells on what it symbolises, aware that the boy has a lot to take in.

"Each of the seven points marked by Hawksmoor's steeples is connected by what we call a *ley line*," he begins. "You can't see them. You simply sense their existence if you're willing to believe. There are said to be hundreds of ley lines crisscrossing the city deep underground, and each end – or *waypoint* – has a corresponding star."

Julius pauses as Yoshi lifts his eyes to the night sky. The boy switches his attention between big stars, bright stars and constellations, staring so intently he can almost see the universe slowly turning.

"So what's the point of these ley lines?" asks Yoshi, sounding a little sceptical.

"In magick circles, it is reckoned that these were once used to deliver energies from one waypoint to the next, sometimes for good reasons and other times for mischief. Nowadays, modern folk send a stroppy fax or a congratulatory email, but this is how they did things when the city was first founded. In this Faerie Ring arrangement, the lines are connected to flow as one. It works as a kind of spiritual electric fence."

"Uh huh." Yoshi tries hard not to smile. "And does it stop the spooks from straying?"

"The ring is intended to keep spooks *out*, Yoshi. Please, dear boy. Just say the word and we'll forget all about it. You can head back and learn all manner of mind tricks and feats that appear to defy reason, but I believe you can offer so much more. The tags around your neck certainly mark you out as a very special boy."

"They do?" Yoshi tries to read the inscription on one, but it's upside down to him and just out of view under his nose. "Do you know what it means?"

"I have an eye for mathematical patterns, Yoshi. All I can say is those numbers are not random."

"Eleven twenty-three?"

"Separate the numbers, dear boy."

Yoshi has a look. "One, one, two and three."

"Correct. Now add the first number to the next, and you'll find the total equals the number that follows."

Yoshi looks again. "One plus one equals two.

"And one plus two equals three."

The boy looks up at Julius. "So what?"

"It's all about connections, dear boy. What we have here is a numerical pattern that flourishes in the natural world. Some even say it's a *sacred* sequence, such is its presence in every aspect of our lives. Observe the seeds in a sunflower head, for example, from the centre to the outer edge, and you'll find the numbers increase by adding the first one to the next and so on. You can find the same pattern in everything from fish scales to snail shells and the structure of petals and leaves. Yoshi, its connection with the universe and everything in it has inspired artists, engineers, musicians and writers for centuries."

"It doesn't inspire much in *me*," says Yoshi, feeling only frustration at his lack of memory. "Then again, I'm not very good with numbers."

"You don't need to be. What we have here are just the first few digits in a sequence that represents the hidden wonders at work on this earth. Indeed, I think we should be looking for a connection between these numbers at its most primitive level."

"And what is that?" asks Yoshi, looking at the engraving on his tag in a very different light now.

"Add the numbers in the sequence together, dear boy. Simple as that."

Yoshi rolls out his bottom lip, thinking this sounds like child's play. "One plus one plus two plus three?" he says to check.

"Indeed."

"That's easy," the boy replies, and then pauses with the answer on his lips. "Seven," he says, quietly. "Seven again."

"The same number as the steeples and the stars. A magical number, interlinked here in a sequence known for its sacred natural properties. Whoever put these tags around your neck knows something about you that we need to crack."

"I know nothing!" protests Yoshi. "Until I woke up in your bunker I wasn't even aware that London *had* seven spooky steeples!"

His comment prompts Julius to glance at his pocket watch, and then promptly curse his time-keeping.

"Quick!" He grabs the telescope, uncaps the lens and invites the boy to look east. "Aim high, between those two steeples."

"You're the boss." Yoshi finds the eyepiece, enjoying himself now. All this talk of sacred force-fields from ancient times makes him feel like a cloak has been lifted from the city. "What am I looking for exactly?"

Julius glances at his pocket timepiece again. "Just watch," he breathes, "and draw your own con-clusions. All I ask is that you keep that mind of yours wide open."

Yoshi focuses the lens. The stars sharpen up accordingly, and then something wipes the smile from his face. Such is his surprise that he breaks away from the eyepiece, as if this is a vision he needs to see with his own eyes.

At first it could almost be a starburst: a point of light out there in the galaxy that suddenly blooms and then fades to black again. But then the dark spot seems to grow, consuming stars around it, and a breeze begins to rise from the east.

"How d'you do that?" the boy gasps, stunned as the inky mass opens up like a sheet and begins winding towards the city. "I can't even see the strings!"

"There are none," whispers Julius. He doesn't take his eyes off Yoshi, as if he's seen it before and knows just what's going to happen. This apparition is so dark it's defined by the stars that blink in and out of sight with every beat of what appear to be *wings*. Assuming a spectral shape, it descends both swiftly and in absolute silence. The stiffening breeze is the only indication that something is heading this way. It's enough to cause the boy's heart to shrink inside his chest. Closer and closer it comes, swooping between the two steeples now, spanning a mile or more. Yoshi is set to scramble back down the ladder but it's too late for that. All he can do is hold his breath and cling to the ledge as a vast shadow glides over the city. The breeze begins to sing in his ears, a wailing opera in the air that sails right over their heads and then decays into the night.

When the boy looks up, he sees only twinkling stars. If there's a dark tail to be seen, it has quickly faded to nothing.

"That's some trick!" cries Yoshi, trying hard not to sound shaken. He looks to street level, hoping to glimpse some of the punks responsible for the illusion he has witnessed. Below, some litter settles in the wake of the wind, while the drunk continues to sing as if nothing untoward has happened. There's nothing else to see or hear.

"It's lucky most people are tucked up in bed at this time," says Julius. "Otherwise there'd be mayhem. There's always the odd report to the police, or a call to some late-night radio phone-in, but anyone who's up at this hour has usually had too much beer or too little sleep to be believed."

"Will you show me how it was done?"

"This time, Yoshi, you need to believe that what you just saw was real." The old man looks up at the sky again, his ears pricking up at the slightest upturn in the breeze. "We should head below ground again. We're safe from harm down there. The greatest trick the devil ever played was to convince us that he ruled the underworld."

"The *devil*?"

Julius flattens his lips behind all those whiskers, still gazing over the rooftops. "London is a place of great significance. It's a major financial capital, a political powerhouse and a cultural beacon to boot. If you had grand designs for global domination, chances are you'd start right here."

Yoshi looks to the skies once more. "So we're number one on the hit list?"

"For the time being London is protected. A force of light flows through the ley lines, as it has since the city's first foundations were laid. It controls the *psyche* of the city, much as the human mind controls all thought, emotion and behaviour."

"You make the place sound like it's living and breathing," declares Yoshi.

"Indeed," replies Julius, seemingly unaware that the boy is finding all this rather hard to take in. "Your psyche is responsible for your mood, if you like, and the ring functions in the very same way. For centuries, the energies coursing around it ensure that this capital is a beacon for prosperity. But should the ring ever fall into the wrong hands, this bunker wouldn't protect us. It might be designed to withstand a nuclear winter, but not the degree of darkness the great Satan could bring to this city."

"Really?" All of a sudden, Yoshi feels cold and exposed. He peers over his shoulder, half expecting to see legions of demons leap the divides between the surrounding buildings. When the boy looks back, the old man is quick to address his fears.

"Yoshi, if the devil ever found his way into this city, he'd be the kind of person you'd pass in the street without a second glance. How else do you think he could operate on the ground? We might be

70

talking about an ancient system of magick here, designed to prevent him from crossing the threshold, but these are modern times. Even if he *did* find a way in, he couldn't just show up sporting cloven hooves, a rakish beard and horns, and nor could he threaten fire and brimstone. It's a jungle out there, after all. The citizens would assume he was just some joker dressed up to run a marathon for charity, or strip off at hen nights and make a bride-to-be blush. Standing out from the crowd like this, he'd be targetted by muggers within minutes. He has to be smarter than that. He has to become a figure of influence within the city, like a politician, a newspaper editor, a rock star, architect or lawyer. He needs to bring out the worst excesses in us all, like greed, lust and selfishness. In short, Yoshi, he has to appear human, like you and I, so that when he brings this city to its knees we might even turn to him for help."

"Now you're scaring me." Yoshi faces up to Julius. "Is this for real?"

"More real than you could imagine, young man. It could begin with anything from the closure of schools and hospitals, a riot outside a concert or the construction of high-rise housing that only the rich could afford . . ." He trails off there for a moment, as a police siren wails through the night. "At first each blow to the city will seem like one of those normal things, but once his minions are recruited from the top down it'll be too late to save the city, let alone yourself. Even those you consider to be your closest friends might conspire to bring you down, or set you up to take a fall that could cause you to suffer for the rest of your life."

"Wow." Yoshi whistles, unsure whether to swallow dryly or dismiss the theory outright. "Someone's done their homework."

"The devil, as they say, is in the detail."

"Can't you cast a spell to make sure the energy stays on our side?" asks Yoshi, sold now on the story and shaken up by it, too.

Julius smiles to himself and caps his telescope. "We can't just wave a wand, dear boy. Stage props like that are vital when it comes to persuading tourists to part with their money, but they have no place here."

"So what *do* we need?" asks the boy, as Julius begins the descent once more.

"Firstly I must ask you not to share this with the others," he says, sinking slowly out of sight. "I don't want to alarm them, and nor do I wish to invite their ridicule. You must return and become a student of their street art, dear boy. Learn a little magic that all of us can master."

"No problem – but as I can't even shuffle cards without dropping them I don't see how I'm going to conjure up a way to keep the devil from this Faerie Ring."

Julius comes to a halt, the lamplight way below him, and peers up at the boy. "The ring's power is locked up in the ley lines. If we're going to keep them safe and sound, what we need is a *key*."

9

HOW WE DO IT

It's first light, at the far end of a dead-end alley, and something stirs among the weeds. A pair of hands appears to sprout through the bars. This is followed by a boy in full bloom, judging by his colourful costume.

Billy No-Beard clenches something tightly between his teeth, but it isn't a cutlass, despite his pirate theme. It's a pair of knotted laces, with two roller-blade boots dangling underneath. He blinks in the early sun, glances around, and then hauls himself up as if boarding a ship.

It may be too early for the tourists, but the din at the mouth of the alley tells Billy the market is open for business. Strapped into his boots now, he sets off past the shuttered kitchen. With his chest puffed, he switches around on his wheels to face the weeds, but doesn't stop moving or even slow down.

"Come out, come out, where*ever* you are!" he sings,

spreading his hands wide. "It's a *beauuuutiful* day for magic and mischief!"

Immediately, another head pops up through the bars. This one is sporting bright red spikes and a scowl. It's Mikhail, and he really doesn't look like he's here to chip in with the chorus.

"*Shush!*" he hisses, and clambers out himself. "Can we please stop showing off?"

Billy brakes with one heel, and folds his arms. "Where is the new boy, anyway?" he asks, as a band of sun-dodging punks crawl out behind Mikhail. All of them are hauling heavy-duty cases of different shapes and sizes. They look like buskers moving an orchestra of instruments, with Billy conducting from the front before anyone is ready. "All I'm trying to do is entertain the crew," he protests. "A little song, to put a spring into their step."

"Billy, honking like that is not entertaining. It's embarrassing!" Mikhail steps away from the weeds, clearing a space for the next arrival. "Any more of that racket and the poor new lad's ears might start bleeding."

At this, Yoshi emerges from the pit, followed by several other kids. "Don't mind me," Yoshi says and grins at his newfound friends. "I'm just keen to find out where I came from." Rising up beside Mikhail now, his attention turns to the buildings pressing in on this cramped alleyway. To his eye, these wonky dwellings seem to almost climb over one another. Yoshi traces an imaginary path from the wall to a sloping gable roof. "Maybe if I climbed up there I'd get my bearings," he says, half thinking of his earlier view of the city.

"I don't think so," scoffs Mikhail. "The rooftops are for pigeons and parkours."

Yoshi looks at him questioningly. "What are they?"

"Pigeons?" he repeats. "Grey-feathered birds with beady eyes. Can't stand them, personally. They give me the creeps."

"*Parkours*, Mikhail! I'm sure I've heard that term before."

"Oh, you know." The Russian boy shrugs. "Those crazy free-runner dudes. The ones who leap from building to building like God should've given them wings. You'd think they have a problem using pavements, the way they head for the rooftops at every opportunity."

"Oh," says Yoshi, none the wiser.

"You see them around town every now and then, but you need to keep your eyes to the sky, and that isn't so easy when what you really want is a spare pair in the back of your head. Having seen who chased you here, Yoshi, my advice is to stay underground with us. Whether you're in the city or the wilderness, you get warmth and protection from a good bolt hole."

"I suppose you're right."

"I *know* I'm right," Mikhail confirms. "I also know that you need food to survive, so let's earn some breakfast."

"Whatever you say." Yoshi raises his hands, pretending to surrender. "You're the boss."

"I wouldn't go that far," warns Mikhail, under his breath. "But if Billy was in charge, we'd all be ordered to dress up like musketeers on wheels."

"What is that all about?" asks Yoshi, speaking up as Billy swings out of earshot. "Is his entire wardrobe fancy dress?"

"Below ground, we can wear whatever we please," says Mikhail. "We're safe from the kind of grief you might get from looking different on the surface. Sure, we might tease one another, but always in good fun. Bullying is banned, you see. As anyone who joins the bunker is usually running away from that kind of trouble, so it's a rule that suits us all."

Mikhail instructs the others to join Billy at the far end, asking for a moment more with Yoshi. "We all have hard-luck tales to tell," he continues, once everyone is out of earshot, "and Billy is a case in point."

"What happened to him?"

"That's a story for Billy to share when he feels you can be trusted," suggests Mikhail. "All I can tell you is that he went through hell before he found himself here. And when he did, boy did he blossom! However Billy chooses to express himself is fine by us, mind you. What matters is that he can keep the bunker shipshape, and cook up a storm for the crew." He pauses there and smacks his lips. "Now, you *must* be hungry, and I don't just mean to learn more about yourself. Follow me, my friend! Let's get on with conjuring up some food."

"Roger that!" laughs Yoshi, mindful of the operation he had witnessed from the control room. At the same time, he can't help but dwell upon what he had been running from when he fell upon the bunker. He hangs back from the Russian boy for a moment, his expression turning thoughtful. When he catches up, he has one last question for him. "If my memory comes back to me, do you think I'll have a hard luck story to tell like everyone else?"

"Who knows?" Mikhail answers as they join the waiting crew. "But if you want a happy ending, you'd be wise to stick with us."

The market here strikes up before dawn, only to close for business before the sightseers begin to tour the streets. Like so much in Chinatown, there's more going on than you might think. If everyone knew the stalls that briefly come to life were crammed with every delicacy known to the Orient, the place would be overrun. And so the chefs and restaurateurs who come here to buy wholesale keep it a secret among themselves. They deal as fast as they can, haggling over packing crates, slapping down money, knocking back coffee, trading jokes, fresh produce, chickens and prize roosters. Occasionally, an early bird might stumble upon this exotic thoroughfare, and wonder how such a glorious bazaar has been missed out from the guidebooks. By the time they return with their friends, however, the traders will have packed up for the day. Instead, they'd find the shutters lifted on the grocery stores, kitchens and medicine houses, with no sign of what has gone before but for the odd stray feather and an unusual spill of spices. Even the pushcarts and packing crates will have vanished into thin air, only to return in the small hours once the tourists have retired to bed.

Right now, such a transformation seems a world away. The place is ablaze with colour and humming with activity. Over there is the chef with the chop knife. The one who had recently come so close to skinning a lost boy on his last legs. He's busy arguing with an elderly herbalist. Every now and then, he breaks away from the display of open pots and bowls to sneeze. Yoshi keeps one eye on him from a safe distance. The boy is standing with Mikhail on the opposite side of the street, beside a telephone box rigged out as a pagoda.

"Don't worry about him now," says Mikhail. "Keep your eye on the operation. You never know when you'll be called upon to help out."

Yoshi refocuses his attention on the rest of the crew. They're still gathered back down the pavement at the alley mouth. Most are sitting on their cases, watching Billy laying cards out on the pavement, while one of the girls stands watch over the market.

"What's with all the luggage?" asks Yoshi curiously.

"Tools of the trade!" declares Mikhail, as if Yoshi should've known this by now. "We can't just conjure up a magic trick out of thin air. We need *props*. Specialist equipment to help persuade our audience that what they're seeing is real. The punters might think they're witnessing miracles. We know it all comes down to military planning and showmanship."

"I see," says Yoshi, his thoughts returning now to the dark spectacle he had witnessed with Julius. What had swept over the city seemed real enough and chilling too. Even the old man's ramblings about Faerie Rings and unlocking ley lines made sense in its wake. His very mention of some quest for a key had certainly struck a chord in the boy, even though he couldn't quite work out why.

But now, in the clear light of day, Yoshi can't help thinking that perhaps he really *has* been duped by some grand illusion. "Mikhail," he asks, still watching the crew, "do you believe in *real* magic?"

"This is as real as it gets," he says. "If the punters can't fathom how we perform our tricks, they have to conclude that what we do must draw upon some higher power."

"So you don't buy all that . . . *mystic* stuff?"

At this, Mikhail turns to face him directly. "The mumbo jumbo that Julius studies? Yoshi, the way I see things, *everything* has an explanation. Take that card trick I showed you. I can't read your mind. I have no special powers. I simply offered you a pack that had been neatly split into red and black cards. I watched you pick a card from the black side, and encouraged you to return it to the red side. I might have then cut the deck a few times, but your card would always be the only single black card sandwiched between two reds."

"Oh!" declares Yoshi. "I get it now. I guess it's quite simple when you think about it."

"Always the way," Mikhail agrees. "Whatever Julius has seen, maybe he just hasn't worked out how it's done."

Yoshi considers this for a moment, wondering whether the old man was a trickster or had simply been fooled himself. At the same time, the girl on watch spots something of interest in the market. She turns to the others and points to the far side of the street.

"What's she seen?" asks Yoshi.

"Breakfast," Mikhail replies, and blows on his hands to keep warm. "See that stall with the green tea urn and the dim sum snacks? The lady behind it is one of our regulars. We try out new tricks on Mae Ling, and in return she gives us discount on all that tasty food."

Yoshi turns his attention towards this short, slight-looking old lady, wrapped up in a big old scarf and quilted coat, and finds she's already noticed him. She waves cheerily, and then again to the crew at the alley mouth.

"She looks like she's expecting us," he says, and waves back awkwardly.

"Oh, Mae has learned to be on the lookout from the moment she opens her stall. Our job is to surprise her, even if she does see us coming."

As he speaks, the phone inside the pagoda starts to ring. Mikhail excuses himself. He reaches in for the receiver, sighing to himself like whoever's on the other end is late. "*Zdravstvuite*," he mutters, then covers the mouthpiece with his palm. "It's Russian for hello," he tells Yoshi with a shrug. "Old habits die hard." He returns to the call, nods and grunts in places, then startles the boy by showing him the handset. "It's for you," he says.

Yoshi looks at him quizzically. "Who is it?" he asks, but Mikhail shrugs like it isn't his business. With a sigh Yoshi takes the phone and presses it to his ear.

"This is the Bridge," pipes a young voice at the other end, sounding even more official than Billy had the day before. *"Do you copy?"*

"Erm, I think so," says Yoshi. "What's up?"

"Listen carefully, soldier. Bravo Team have requested that you remain in this position until further notice. Under no circumstances should you put down the phone. Is that clear? Do not. Put down. The phone!"

Yoshi turns to Mikhail for advice, barely believing what he has just heard. The Russian boy winks at him, and begins to back away. At the same time, Billy and several crew members advance, clutching two of the longest reinforced cases. With professional ease, they set them down on the pavement, flip open the latches, and remove two full-length mirrors. The boy is lost for words, watching, with the phone still pressed to his ear, as they prop a mirror behind a stall. It's facing the wall behind the phone box he's in, reflecting nothing but bricks. Next, one of the crew crouches down and carefully tilts the mirror towards the mystified boy with the handset pressed to his ear.

Meantime, Billy and a scruffy-looking lad bring the second mirror towards him. It covers the front of the box perfectly, from side to side and top to bottom.

"What's going on?" breathes Yoshi down the line, as Billy tilts the mirror towards the one behind the stall. Yoshi turns without thinking, and promptly gets cobbled in the phone cable. "I can't see out!"

"The trial run is almost complete," assures the voice on the line. *"In a moment I'll patch you across to Mikhail. He's wired up with a microphone as well as an earpiece, so you'll know when your time has come."*

"Huh?" Yoshi doesn't like the sound of this one bit. He draws breath to complain, only for sunlight to slide across him once again as Billy and the boy shift the mirror clear. "Where are they going now?"

"Just relax, soldier. You're doing good." Yoshi looks out once more, seeking some kind of explanation from Mikhail. This time, he spots him on the opposite side of the crowded market street. Mikhail is talking to Mae Ling in front of her stall. He looks kind of animated, making shapes with his hands as he talks. *"The distraction process is almost complete. All you have to do is keep talking and be cool."*

"What are you going to do with me?" asks Yoshi, trying hard not to sound panicked. "Will it hurt?"

"So long as you follow instructions," the voice assures him, *"you won't feel a thing."*

10

OUT OF HERE

The way Yoshi feels, left hanging on the line like this, he might as well be under a spotlight. Billy is standing to one side with the second mirror, out of sight from Mae Ling. He catches Yoshi looking at him, and touches a finger to his lips. The phone feels hot against his ear, while the hairs on the back of his neck begin to prickle. For one horrible moment, he wonders if the entire phone box might suddenly soar into the sky like some kind of infernal elevator. Another crackle brings his fears back to ground level. Then a Russian voice clips in through the receiver that prompts Yoshi to focus on Mikhail across the road.

"... and that, Mae Ling, is how it's possible to survive in a glass box for over a month without food. Now, my crew like our grub too much to get involved in that kind of stunt, so how about we earn ourselves something to eat with a little trick of our own."

"Sure thing, Mikhail. But you won't fool me so easy.

I bring my glasses today, see?" The old lady is wearing a pair of half-moon spectacles on a chain around her neck. From the box, Yoshi watches her prop them on her nose. *"OK, what you got me?"*

"Let me begin by introducing you to a new friend." Mikhail steps aside and gestures over the market strip towards the phone box. *"Yoshi there has lost his memory. He's making a quick call to report it missing. We're just worried it's not only his memory that's in danger of vanishing."*

"I know this." Mae Ling claps her hands together. *"You got false bottom in that phone booth. Am I right? I turn around. The stooge drops out of sight."*

"Oh, please!" Mikhail sounds wounded. *"Do we look like amateurs? You know us, Mae Ling. If we can't do a job properly, we don't do it at all. We could make our boy there disappear in a blink, but let's think bigger than that. What do you say we make the whole box vanish into thin air?"*

"I say you crazy boys!" She sounds both dismissive and delighted. *"Go ahead then, Mikhail. Make my day!"*

"Very well," Yoshi hears him say, and his grip tightens around the receiver. *"But first you've got to let me taste one of those dumplings."*

"Hey, hands off!" Mae Ling laughs as Mikhail reaches for one of the small snacks without warning, and playfully slaps his wrist. It's the moment the crew have been waiting for. In a blink, Billy and

his boy have snapped the mirror into place in front of the phone box. Swiftly they tilt it towards the mirror behind the stall, just as they have practised, and then scurry out of sight.

The move leaves Yoshi unable to see the old woman across the street. Even so, he doesn't need the phone to hear the cry of delight that follows, and judge from it that the trick has worked a treat. *"How you do that, Mikhail? Where is the phone box? All I see are bricks!"*

Yoshi glances at the boy with the other mirror, still hiding from Mae Ling. He's tilted it now to reflect the wall behind them onto the mirror in front of the box. He certainly looks very pleased with himself, as he's managed to seamlessly blend the reflected brickwork with the real thing. Yoshi can't help grinning himself, especially when he hears Mae Ling protest again. For as Mikhail helps himself to yet more dim sum, he signals on the sly for the removal of the props around the box.

With the mirrors gone, Yoshi is free to see his friend pop another snack in his mouth, then face him directly.

"Look who's back, Mae Ling!" he says, feigning surprise.

The old lady turns, peels off her glasses to check the lenses haven't deceived her, and then takes a step back.

"You did it! Wowee, Mikhail. You earned big breakfast today. Take all the grub you can eat!"

Yoshi waves at them both, relieved to have come through the illusion unscathed. Billy and the rest of the crew look just as pleased. Even so, something doesn't feel quite right to the boy. The hairs on the back of his neck are still prickling wildly. He glances around, sees nothing strange – just people browsing and striking deals – and yet his heart continues to hammer. He'd almost be able to hear it beating away, but a high-pitched hum has started up in his ears. It sounds like some kind of interference, and yet nobody else in the market seems to notice. Yoshi winces, feeling both confusion and alarm. Then, out of nowhere, a flash appears to go off in front of him. He blinks and shields his eyes on impulse, only to realise that the flash has come from within. And as it fades away, taking with it the piercing noise, he is left with the weird but unmistakeable impression of two tight blue eyes. Slowly a face and then a figure take shape in his mind, flanked by ornate gates just like those that book-end this very street. A static click down the line spells an end to this dreamlike vision. It's Mission Control, congratulating him.

"You did good, soldier. You can stand down now, and stuff your face."

"Something's wrong," is all Yoshi can say. He

blinks until his focus sharpens on his surroundings once again. The image in his mind has gone, but not the sense of foreboding.

"No problems reported from here. The target can't believe what she's just seen, so who's complaining? You're kinda new at this game to be a perfectionist."

Yoshi is about to explain that it isn't the illusion that concerned him. Then his eyes lock onto a figure through the crowd, and open wide in dread.

The brute in the white mink coat prowls from one stall to the next. He's entirely bald, with a neck so thick it folds at the back, and a brow at the front like a rock face. His sheer presence is impossible to ignore, from his height to his giant build. The boy watches him pick over the produce on offer, and barely breathes at this shock sighting. His memory might not go back much further than the fog-bound night in which he arrived, but he's certain this guy is very bad news.

"It's him," he croaks into the phone. "He's come back for me."

A pause crackles down the line. The sound of the Bridge in confusion. *"Soldier, you look a little unwell. Your order is to return to the bunker."*

Yoshi cannot stop gawping at the man in the mink. He's obviously arrived in search of some-thing, but it's clear he hasn't spotted Yoshi. Then he stops, right beside Mikhail, in front of Mae Ling's stall. He's drawn, it seems, just like the Russian boy, to the tasty-looking snacks on display.

"Oh no!" Yoshi freezes at what follows. For Mae Ling is still making an almighty song and dance about the vanishing act that's just been pulled off in her honour. It's enough to distract anyone currently picking over her produce, until they decide to see what all the fuss is about. Slowly the brute turns around. And for the second time in a matter of moments, Yoshi comes face to face with a pair of baleful, blue eyes. This time, they seem to bore right through the boy for real.

"Get me out of here," he yells down the line. "Now!"

"*Huh?*" The voice from the Bridge doesn't sound so in charge this time.

"The mirrors!" breathes Yoshi urgently, just as the man in the mink begins to push across the crowd. The market is at its busiest, however, and for a moment Yoshi loses sight of him. When he spots the brute among the throng again he's closer still. This time, however, he's looking angered by all the people in his way.

"Please," the boy yells into the phone, "get the mirrors back in place!" Just then a squeal causes heads in the crowd to turn, upon which two porters attempt to push through. They're shouting at one another, and seem to be in pursuit of something at ground level. Amid the chaos, the crowd on Yoshi's side open up, and a loose pig scurries out. "Now!" he screams, seizing this last opportunity. "Make me disappear!"

Billy No-Beard is there with the mirror in an instant. He's evidently trained to act without question. Even so, the look he shoots Yoshi before covering the phone box makes it clear that he's confused.

"Both mirrors are in place, soldier. Do you want to tell us what this is about?"

"The guy in the street," Yoshi whispers, unable to see out himself now. "The big bald monster with the fancy coat. What's he doing?"

"Scratching his big bald head," comes the response after a moment. *"He looks a little lost."*

"What else?"

"He's looking in your direction, and frowning hard. Oh . . . hold on."

"What?"

"He's heading your way!"

"But I'm stuck! You have to help! It's the guy who was after me the other night. He's coming to get me and I'm trapped!"

"Calm down, soldier. He's stopped again. People are flocking across to see what all the squealing and shouting was about just now. The target is trying to steer around them but he isn't getting far."

91

"Are you sure he can't see me? Are the mirrors reflecting the brick wall behind this box?"

"*Of course they are! We're professional street magicians, not hucksters! I can't speak for the little piggy, but it seems you might just get away with this. The target is looking in your direction again, but there's nothing to see. The illusion works a treat so long as nobody walks behind the box, and Billy has been briefed to stop that from happening.*"

"You guys think of everything," says Yoshi.

"*You don't need spells to make magic, soldier. Just thorough planning— hang on, there's another swell of people in his way . . . That's it! He's giving up trying to cross to your side of the street. He doesn't look happy, but you're in the clear.*"

"Are you certain?"

"*Seems he's lost his appetite for dim sum, too. If you want me to carry on tracking him I'm going to have to switch traffic cams.*"

"You mean he's leaving?"

"*Affirmative, soldier. Target has exited the market. Looks like we made you vanish in the nick of time.*"

A second later, a sound shoots up over the market like a firework. Those people passing Mae Ling's stall turn in the direction of the noise, only to carry on about their business because there's nothing to be seen. Just a worn-looking brick wall behind the stalls, though some might swear that a phone box

92

usually stands there. There's certainly something fishy about this scene. For as everybody knows, brick walls don't whoop in relief.

11

WHO AM I?

Back in the bunker, the Canteen is buzzing with chatter and the clink of cutlery. Nearly every place is taken along the benches. Even Julius Grimaldi eats with the crew, though he doesn't pause to join in the conversation. He looks like someone plugged into a personal music player with the volume set to max. Despite the noise and excitement, he appears totally tuned out of what's going on around him.

The street team have returned, along with several other crews dispatched around town to make magic this morning. Mae Ling has certainly rewarded them well. But by all accounts, the stunt over at Smithfield's Meat Market has earned the biggest feast of them all. Right now, the crew responsible are dining out on their success, reliving the story in between mouthfuls of hot, salt-beef bagels. They're midway through the tale, bragging about how they had gathered a crowd of butchers in bloodstained aprons and persuaded a porter to hand over his wedding ring in front of them. First they appeared to make it disappear into thin air. Next they invited his associate to slice open the belly of a pig carcass that the pair had been hoping to sell on the side. It's gruesome stuff, but they had read their audience well.

"You should've seen their faces when he pulled out the ring!" one boy pipes up. "Each porter had bet twenty quid on such a feat being impossible. Not only did they lose, some market official then stepped out of the crowd and issued a fine for unlicensed trading."

"Serves them right for being so greedy," shouts another.

"Think of the pig!" chimes a wag from the back of the canteen. "Sounds like it was proper gutted!"

Only Julius fails to join in with the laughter and uproar that follows. He smiles at their high spirits, but carefully pats his mouth with his napkin, then makes a quiet exit. For one crew member is missing, and this well-mannered old man doesn't need to be a mind-reader to work out why.

"I heard you had another narrow escape, dear boy."

Yoshi jumps and turns in surprise, just as Julius had expected. The old man hangs back from the lad, standing in the open doorway as he has for some minutes. The new arrival is alone in the Bridge, facing the giant screen at the front. The lights are on dim. The panels twinkle dreamily, but there's no live action on the monitor banks. Most are switched off. The few that are still blazing show a video-game menu for some online tournament that has yet to kick off.

"I haven't touched anything," says Yoshi, and shows his hands.

"I don't blame you," Julius replies. "I wouldn't dare to mess with their settings, and frankly I don't care to, either. Technology has rather run away with itself on the surface. At least the things you find by digging down relate to the past and not the future. It means you know where you are, no matter how low you go."

He joins Yoshi, drawing level to take in the big screen. The shot displayed is on freeze. It shows an overhead view of the main market drag, taken by one of the crowd-control cams just after the crew had made the phone box vanish.

"I know where I am, all right," the boy says eventually. "I just really need to find out where I started." He nods towards the image, the last one taken before the Bridge had declared the morning's operation closed. The bald-headed ogre in the coat dominates the frame, despite all the people in it.

"I may not be able to remember anything, but I do know that my friend here wants me back."

"Seems so." Julius twiddles with the tip of his beard. "Had we known he was lurking, we could've shadowed him. Some of the crew can creep right up on a person and stick to them like glue. Shadowing is a handy talent when it comes to planting cards or picking wallets."

"Everyone here has some cool skills," says Yoshi. "But I doubt any of them would dare to get too close to this guy."

The pair fall silent. The moment in time captured up there says it all. With his back to the camera, moving against the crowd, the man in the mink looks like he is all set to cut an easy path for himself. It's as if the people he's facing have taken one look at him and stepped aside to let him through.

"If I were unfortunate enough to witness him stomping towards me," observes Julius finally, "I'd make myself scarce too."

"I saw him coming," says Yoshi quietly, and glances at the old man.

"I don't doubt it. You can hardly miss a monster like him."

"You misunderstand me." Yoshi faces him directly, and taps the side of his head. "I saw him coming – in here. Really. I know it sounds ridiculous, but I had a clear vision just seconds before he showed up.

It was overwhelming, as if I had a bird's-eye view of something I couldn't possibly see."

Julius Grimaldi considers what Yoshi has just said. He tips his head to one side and touches his lips with one finger. "It doesn't sound ridiculous," is his first response. "In fact, dear boy, it makes perfect sense. Didn't I tell you those tags around your neck marked you out as special?" Julius brings his hands together and his eyes seem to brighten behind his spectacles. "The gift of foresight and premonition is something the boys and girls inside this bunker can only *pretend* to pull off, Yoshi. With you, I think we're only scratching the surface when it comes to your true gifts."

"Well, I know how to make myself invisible," Yoshi confesses, "but I need a couple of mirrors first."

"This is about more than illusions, my boy. This is about the power of the human *mind*! That you can see things before they happen is impressive. It tells me you're tuned in to a higher natural wavelength than the rest of us – though, of course, you're not the first. Throughout history, individuals have tapped in to psychic energies, and we're not talking about the toothless old crones who have fooled themselves into believing they can read tea leaves and crystal balls."

"The fortune-tellers are an act?" Yoshi looks

at him in surprise. "No offence, Julius, but a trip to the fairground with you must be kind of a let-down."

"Yoshi," he continues firmly. "I'm talking about upstanding members of society. Figures through time who have drawn upon their powers and stamped their mark on the world!"

The boy thinks about this for a second, and frowns. "Are they magicians?"

"Magicians who work with bricks and mortar," agrees Julius. "Indeed, there are many buildings conjured up within these city walls that have cast a spell on us all for centuries. You saw some for yourself last night."

"The seven churches?"

"Each with a steeple that together forms a very special shape, all thanks to the architect and vision-ary, Nicholas Hawksmoor."

"He saw things?"

"Oh yes. Hawksmoor saw a great many things. He secretly devoted his life's work to marking out the forces at work around this city."

"The Faerie Ring. I remember that."

"And I doubt you will ever forget it if I'm right about your potential, young man. You see, the ring must always rely on guardians if it is to continue to work as the founding fathers intended. By erecting a church on every waypoint in the ring,

Hawksmoor was basically flagging up where to find it." He sweeps his hand towards the door. "Come with me. It's high time we put your talents to the test."

For a minute or so after they leave, the Bridge lies empty. Lights blink idly from one panel to the next, ticking over, it seems. A familiar rumble precedes the appearance of Billy No-Beard. He arrives with two other crew members in tow. The three fan out across the rows. Each boy takes up position behind a screen, and then summons up the same game menu.

"Man your posts, me hearties." Billy begins to peck at his own keyboard, not once looking at his monitor. Automatically, the spotlights above each boy's station warm up. "Let me remind you this is an online tournament with some of the finest clans competing. I don't want any pussyfooting about, trying to reload your weapons, is that clear? We can't afford to waste our firepower. So, get in there and take down anything that moves. Give it all you've got. Shotguns. Nail guns. Rail guns. The works!"

"Calm down," says the boy to his left. "It's only a soccer tournament."

Billy No-Beard stops typing in the start-up commands, and looks up sharply. On his screen, the virtual players are taking their positions on the pitch. "I knew that," he covers after a moment. "I was talking tactics."

"Oh, sure you were." His wingman opposite grins knowingly. "Gaming isn't all blood and guts, you know. You really should get out more, Billy. See some of the real world for a change." He nods at the big screen as if to illustrate his point, and then checks out the shot of the market. "Isn't that the weirdo who's been stalking our new arrival?"

"Yep, that's the guy. I wonder what Yoshi did to make him so mad?" Billy seems relieved to move away from the gaming screen for a moment. "We had to move fast to get that mirror zigzag back in place, I can tell you. If we'd messed up, I reckon a gorilla like this would've uprooted the whole phone box with Yoshi in it, slung it over his shoulder and marched off just like that."

"If he shows up again I expect Julius will order us to shadow him," says the boy to Billy's left. "You can count me out as a volunteer."

"Wise words," his other wingman agrees. "There's stealth, and then there's sheer stupidity."

"Fellas," says Billy, sitting back as if to referee them now. "Can we stop being such a pair of panty-waists? There's no need to trail him to find out where he came from. We can do it from here, no sweat."

"But he'll be long gone by now," says the boy on his left.

"And in so doing he will have passed under a string of closed-circuit cameras. The police at Scotland Yard record everything and keep it for a short period of time. Just in case a crime is committed and they need the evidence. That means we can track him by tape, without risk of being beaten to a pulp."

The wingmen glance at one another, and then watch as Billy unfreezes the street-cam image on the big screen. He jabs at several keys, and suddenly the crowd move in treble time. Billy toggles through different cameras, catching up with their quarry. And when he does, all three are silenced by a remarkable effect.

For the man in the mink appears to move out of sync with the world around him. The images are stuttered and speeded up, the pedestrians scuttling like ants. And yet through every frame the subject under observation leaves a blurred trail of his own image.

"There must be a fault," mutters Billy to himself. "The camera never lies, unless it's on the blink."

"Unless we're looking at some kind of spectre," quips one lad, and then falls quiet when nobody laughs along with him.

12

KNOW YOUR STRENGTH

The breeze warns Yoshi that a tube train is approaching. It picks up just ahead of a distant tremor, and sweeps out of the tunnel like some spirit taking flight.

"You'll get used to it," says Julius, peering down at the tracks. The pair are midway across a lattice footbridge, at one end of a platform last used as a shelter during the Blitz. A *ghost* station, is what Yoshi's guide called it. One of several dozen, he had estimated, dotted and deserted under the city. The pair are leaning against the handrail, with the lamp at their feet. The candlelight flickers and then bends away, the wind strengthening all the while. The old man faces the boy, his unkempt hair blowing across his face now. "Sometimes you'll see maintenance gangs spill out of the tunnel long before this blessed gale begins to even breathe. Those guys know how to recognise the warning signs, as you will too if you spend enough time with us."

"There's certainly a lot to discover," agrees Yoshi, looking around.

Along the length of the platform, the walls are lined with peeling posters inviting young men to sign up for a war. Soot is piled under the benches, blown back by the trains that still pass through but never stop. Yoshi braces himself as the rails begin to flex and twang, the volume building all the time. "These maintenance gangs," he asks. "If they don't wait for the wind, how do they know when a train is coming?"

With a chuckle, Julius Grimaldi holds the lamp over the rail. Down below, dark shapes scurry among the rails. "The rats!" he declares. "If you're underground and you hear the patter of tiny feet, get out as fast as you can. Don't wait for the wind rush," he warns, and leans across to be heard as the head of a train slams out of the tunnel. *"It's too late by then!"*

Had Yoshi ventured this far from the bunker alone, he would've been lost at the first turn. From a big old water main, dripping with stalactites, they had crawled into a short tunnel that led to a plundered bank vault blown open on both sides. From there, the pair had swung out into an abyss on a thick, knotted rope and descended to a dark and silted shoreline at low tide. Finally, a short climb through an air ventilation shaft had delivered them onto this long-forgotten platform. Yoshi might have had much to fear from this journey, but Julius picked his way across town with great purpose. Indeed, the boy figured he had only paused here to watch the train clatter under their feet, but the old man doesn't move on as expected.

"Is there much further to go?" asks Yoshi. "My back is hurting from so much stooping."

"That's one advantage of growing older," replies Julius. "At my age, the stoop comes naturally." Yoshi lifts both arms and stretches, appreciating the space, only to brush the brickwork with his fingertips. A little soot drizzles onto the pair. Yoshi steps away, brushing his shoulder, but Julius seems unfazed. He peers up, hoists the lamp high, and says, "Anyway, it seems we have arrived."

"We have?" Yoshi glances one way then the other, wondering what he's missed out on. "So, where's the church?"

"Oh, way above us on the surface," says Julius, and invites the boy to take a closer look at the vaulted ceiling. The old man brushes at it himself. As more soot falls away, so a familiar pattern takes shape.

The Faerie Ring. Seven lines scratched roughly into the darkest of bricks.

"Did you do this?" asks Yoshi.

105

"I'm an urban explorer," Julius replies, sounding almost offended, "not a vandal. I discovered the same pattern under every church, some in crypts, others deeper down in spaces such as this. It leads me to conclude that each one marks a waypoint between ley lines."

Yoshi cranes his neck, studying the sooty pattern. "It doesn't look like much."

"Maybe the architect didn't want to make a big song and dance about it, Yoshi. There's nothing to see, as such, anyway. It's all in the mind, until you can open the connection between this point and the next."

"Right," says Yoshi. "And how is that done?"

"It's a mystery to me," Julius confesses, "but I believe *you* may be able to shed a little light on things. Tell me what you're feeling right now, Yoshi. Do you sense anything unusual?"

"Just an aching spine," he says.

"Try touching the Faerie Ring."

With a sigh, Yoshi reaches up on tiptoe and presses a fingertip to the brick. It feels cold, damp and gritty, but that's all he has to report.

"Nothing," he says, sounding strained, and comes down onto the soles of his feet.

Julius tries hard not to look crestfallen. "Not even a tingle?" he asks.

"Not even that." Yoshi rubs his hands to clean

them, only to gasp at what falls away. For it's as if the soot has broken up into atoms, and come alive in a shower of colour. These flecks tinkle like wind chimes, and glitter in the lamplight. Most strikingly of all, they appear to move one step behind gravity.

"Good Lord!" Julius drops to one knee and holds out his palm to catch some. On contact, the flecks immediately darken and fade. The old man pushes a finger through what remains. It leaves a dark, sooty smear. He rubs his hand as Yoshi has, sees only blackened brick-dust drop away.

"What have I done?" asks Yoshi, his eyes wide with wonder.

The old man rises to his feet again. "It isn't what you've done," he beams. "It's what you're *capable* of doing that fascinates me. Why don't we try again? This time, focus on the next waypoint." He gestures at the tunnel from which the last train had appeared. "By my reckoning, the nearest Hawksmoor church is half a mile due south from here. If I remember rightly, the Faerie Ring under that one is carved into the bed of a shallow, freshwater brook."

"Should I focus on that?" asks Yoshi, still shaken up by what has just happened.

"My boy, you can focus on whatever comes to mind. The beauty of ancient mysticism is the fact that it really is very simple, and yet we have barely begun to understand it. All we can do here is recognise that there are powerful energies running in a ring under the city. Touching this waypoint has given us a taster. Now we need to find a way to tap right into it."

"You make it sound easy," says Yoshi. He looks up again at the pattern scratched into the brick.

"Just let it flow through you, my boy. Forget about spells and strange brews. This is about having some faith in abilities you never knew you possessed!"

"If you say so." Yoshi cracks his knuckles before trying again. "I'll think watery thoughts, even though it'll probably make me want to pee."

He reaches up, touches the cold stone. A little soot drifts free, but this time it stays quite black. With his eyes squeezed shut, Yoshi tries hard to imagine a bubbling brook. In response, he feels a breath of air on his face, and another distant tremor.

"There's a train coming," he says, struggling now to stay on tiptoe. "Maybe we should wait."

"Just focus on the brook," says Julius to remind him. "Try touching the ring with both hands. See if that helps."

"This is crazy," says Yoshi, but does so anyway.

The breeze strengthens once again, but now the boy has summoned up a clear image – *water*. Lots of it. He can almost hear it in his mind, in fact. Growing louder like the incoming train.

"Oh dear," says Julius quietly.

"What is it?" Yoshi opens his eyes. The image he has conjured up disappears. Unlike the sound of a crashing deluge.

He glances at Julius, unsure whether his ears are playing tricks. It's the look in his eyes that tells the boy this is no illusion. For what they can hear is crystal clear now, and rising behind the rattle of the incoming train.

The pair turn to face the tunnel. The thunder is still building within, and sounds unusually loud. They can even feel it. Soot sieves over the platform, dislodged from the bricks. Even the footbridge starts to shake. With a tightening sense of dread, Yoshi grips the rails with both hands. He glances at Julius, who struggles to keep a brave face. He smiles nervously, as if this kind of thing is an everyday occurrence, but his wide eyes say it all.

Just then, two headlights tilt out of the dark semicircle – coming out of nowhere, it seems. Yoshi sees the driver behind the train's windshield. He could be at the controls of a runaway, judging by his expression. The boy only steals a glimpse of his hounded-looking eyes, before the train thunders under the footbridge. It's what follows that explains his terror.

"Hold on!" yells Julius, the tails of his patchwork jacket flapping behind him now.

The first drops spray forth around the middle carriages, and then comes the surge – filling the tunnel from top to bottom. In a blink, the tube train looks more like a ride in a log flume. Foaming water laps at the platform and the train windows, spitting at the two figures watching, aghast, from above. And yet it isn't the flood that takes their breath away so much as the shoals of pulsing colours shot through it.

They could be looking at creatures from the deep, the way these blobs of light spiral with the current. It's enough to illuminate the space they're in, and wash the tiled walls with dazzling hues. The final carriage ploughs underneath the footbridge just then, trailing two fins of spray. They might as well be looking at white rapids, such is the water's ferocity. The old man yells something about getting away, but as he does so the din from the passing train begins to drop. As does the weird light, followed by the torrent, which skids into shallows and then pools to a halt.

With his heart in his mouth, Yoshi watches the ballast bed gleaming under the lamplight. The stones crackle as the water drains away, and then silence is restored. A ghost station at rest once again.

"So we need a little practise," admits Julius with a shrug. "There was definitely some energy going on there. We just could've done without the rest of it!" He brushes a speck of soot from his lapel, and smiles sheepishly. "At least we didn't get our feet wet."

13

SUN IN MY EYES

Everyone learns new tricks through life. From the moment we're born, it's vital that we pick up how to smile, crawl, talk and walk if we want to survive. Once we've mastered the basics, all kind of stunts can tickle our fancy. It may not be much – like working out how to squeeze the last curl of tooth-paste from the tube, or whistling, using two fingers. Even in such small ways, it can be deeply satisfying to sense that we have pushed ourselves. For a brief moment, it helps us to feel special.

Discovering you have a unique gift is a differ-ent story altogether. You might feel special, but it doesn't guarantee you'll feel good too. If your trick defies all nature and reason, it can leave you wondering where on earth it came from – and what you're supposed to do with it now.

What just happened in the ghost station is a very big deal. This is clear from the way Julius Grimaldi chatters about the episode as he retraces their

112

footprints along the dark, sludgy riverbank. It's also evident from the fact that Yoshi remains silent. He follows the old man with his head down and arms tightly folded, as if keeping his hands from making mischief. It's cold down here, and damp. The silt is thick and sucks at their shoes, but Yoshi looks as if he's brooding on other matters. Julius holds the lantern high. He's so caught up in reliving the moment when that supernatural surge of water washed through the tunnel that he doesn't once turn to check on his young charge.

Right now, in fact, something could surface quietly in the black water beside the boy – say, a snout, two beady eyes, a scaly back and tail – and he just would not notice. Indeed, when Julius hisses *"What was that noise?"* and swings the light out over the river, Yoshi promptly bumps right into him.

"There!" The old man points at the water, but there's nothing to see. Just an eddy turning oddly against the current, which swiftly tapers away. "Did you see it?" he asks. "Something *big!*"

Yoshi shrugs, pushes his hands into his pockets. "Perhaps you imagined it," he suggests. "I expect when I get back up into the real world, I'll find it hard to believe some of the things going on down here."

With a sympathetic sigh, Julius brings the boy into the light of his lamp. "You should be very proud of yourself," he tells him. "Unlocking ley lines is a rare gift. We might have peeped at some surprises, but there's so much more to see. Whoever controls the ring controls London's psyche, remember. For the sake of the city, what we need to find out is whether you really have that ability."

"There's a *lot* I need to find out," mutters Yoshi. What happened had amazed him, but also stirred up a sense of great frustration. The mystery of his background just couldn't be ignored. Something from his past must explain how he could summon a deluge through a tube tunnel just by thinking about water, and why a bald-headed brute in a white mink coat was hellbent on tracking him down. And yet without his memory, the boy remains lost to himself. Until the missing pieces from his personal puzzle appear, thinks Yoshi with a sense of resignation, he must remain dependent on this wise but deeply weird old man in front of him.

"We should keep moving," suggests Julius, as the water stirs again. "The surface dwellers have a saying, you know. They believe that wherever you are in London, a rat is never more than a metre away."

"Is that true?" asks Yoshi, and decides it might be best to keep up with the old man.

"Maybe on the surface." Julius steers him towards the top of the shoreline where the climbing rope awaits. He reaches for the lowest knot, only to glance nervously behind them with his lamp-light. "Down here it isn't just rats you need to watch out for."

Gingerly, Yoshi picks his way from one knot in the rope to the next. Unwilling to look over his shoulder now, especially after what his guide has just shared, he focuses instead on the climb. Hand over hand, foot over foot, he follows Julius without a word, and dwells upon the matter. The rope appears to be tethered high above them. Indeed, he can just make out a small, slotted square of daylight up there. It might well take him to ground level, and even a place called home, if only he knew which way to turn at the top.

Despite this glimpse of the outside world, Yoshi is mightily relieved to leave the rope on reaching the gash in the bank vault. As the boy hauls himself to safety, his dog tags strike the ragged concrete ledge. He glances at the nickel plates dangling from his neck, and then at the old man's walking boots, right there under his nose.

"Take my hand," offers Julius, reaching for him.

The boy looks up, but chooses to stand without help.

"When you first saw this chain around my neck," says Yoshi, testing it between his fingertips, "you said I was lucky to be alive. You also told me it was

115

a blessing that I couldn't remember what I had escaped from."

"Did I?" Julius looks momentarily surprised. "Oh, so I did."

"Julius, you've shown me a hidden side to this city that you know more about than most. I'm thinking you also know more about me than I can remember. If there's *anything*," the boy pleads, "then surely I have a right to be told?"

Julius focuses on the floor. When he looks back, levelling with the boy, it's clear he has a confession to share. "You're not the first lost soul to come here with tags," he says quietly. "And I doubt you'll be the last, either."

Yoshi stares at the old man, burning to know more. This news threatens to knock the boy right out of the hole and onto the riverbed below, but he remains stock still, waiting for more. "Go on," he whispers finally.

"It happened long ago," sighs Julius. "Years before any of this crew arrived. In fact, I seem to remember this vault was state of the art at the time. A seemingly impenetrable fortress where playboys and royalty stashed their valuables." He turns with the lamp, casting light around this long-forgotten space. All the deposit boxes in here have been plundered. Many of the trays hang open, some still feathered by bank notes. As if to demonstrate that this isn't worth getting excited about, the old man prods at a nest of old money, which promptly crumbles to dust. What doesn't give way is the upturned safe, which Julius perches on now to face Yoshi directly. "You remind me of that kid in many ways," he continues. "He had the same fierce sense of determination, and dog tags just like yours. The only difference was the number sequence, and the fact that he didn't knock himself out when he arrived."

"So he knew where he had come from?"

"And he didn't want to go back. *Ever*."

Yoshi swallows uncomfortably. "And where was that?"

"I swear by the seven steeples, I do not know the exact location. He was a freaked-out kid, Yoshi. He couldn't even speak. Every time he tried to find his voice, the words just vaporised. The poor lad clearly knew how to talk, but something had left him mute. We provided him with shelter and food, of course, and a chance to get back on his feet. Indeed, over time he ventured out to practise street magic with the crew. He even incorporated mime into his act, and learned to make an audience howl the way he clowned around with his cards. It was only when he showed us a special trick of his own that we found out what had caught his tongue . . ."

"Go on," says Yoshi, when the old man falls silent himself.

"He started making sketches," he says eventually. "Lots of them."

"What's so special about that?"

"He didn't draw what was in front of him, or even make stuff up." Julius breaks off there, taking a deep breath for what follows: "When this lost soul put pencil to paper in the bunker, he could picture what was happening above us at precisely the same time. Yoshi, this kid was like a human street cam. We would send a crew out to perform in Covent Garden, and he could sketch us what they were up to without any access to a monitor. He could pinpoint their precise location on a map, and even scratch out a portrait of what the target looked like."

"This kid," Yoshi says suddenly. "Did these visions come to him in a weird kind of flash?"

Julius narrows his eyes, reading him closely. "This has happened to you, hasn't it?"

Yoshi reaches for his dog tags. Nervously, he rubs a plate between his thumb and forefinger, then decides to share an account of the two strange moments when the man in the mink had come to mind. "It feels like the sun in my eyes," he explains. "It blinds me to everything, then this clear image of him comes through. The last time it happened, in the market, he showed up for real just seconds

118

later. It really did feel like I had seen him coming."

Julius nods to himself, stroking his whiskers as if his suspicions have been confirmed. "The flash you describe is often reported by people with your gift. I would imagine it's a kind of psychic surge that occurs as the mind's eye opens. It's known as remote viewing."

Yoshi grins, despite himself. "*Remote viewing*?" he repeats, stressing each word. "Isn't that what kids do from the sofa when it comes to switching channels on the telly?"

"The boy who came under our wing didn't need a screen or a control unit," says Julius gravely. "Nor did he feel safe sitting about in one place for too long, which is why he took off from us before we'd had a chance to help him. The powers that be all over the world are fascinated by this unexplained phenomenon. It makes anyone with this ability quite a catch. Some remote viewers might be able to 'see' into a nearby street, which is what happened when your man in the mink coat came to mind. Others have been known to reach across *continents* and pinpoint details with frightening clarity. It might be a lost child, a hostage in a farmhouse or a military base. There have even been rare cases of remote viewers visiting other planets in the solar system, and describing the terrain there before the first satellites have beamed back pictures to confirm it."

"Wow!" Yoshi whistles, still unsure whether to believe what he is hearing, but impressed nonetheless. "The man in the mink might count as my worst nightmare, but I don't think he's come all the way from Mars."

"The mute boy's powers allowed him to visualise things around the city," continues Julius, "but then, like you, he was young and showed potential. Judging by some of the sketches he did for me, it was clear people thought he had a long way to go."

"So what did they show?" asks Yoshi, pawing anxiously at his tags. "These sketches?"

Julius looks to his lap, sighs deeply, and then rises to his feet. "They showed enough for me to keep them to myself," he says. "I didn't want to alarm the crew, you see. For if they'd known what scared him so, they might have feared that their days in the bunker would be numbered."

"Take me to these pictures," demands Yoshi. "Wherever you're hiding them, I need to see them right now."

14

IN THE PICTURE

"Play it again please, Billy."

Mikhail is lying on his back in the Bridge, directly beneath the big screen. A panel hangs loose from the underbelly. Up inside, he's tinkering with circuit boards as thin as wafers. Only his lower legs are visible, and also a hand that reaches out every now and then for a screwdriver or soldering iron. The two boys who had been hoping to get to grips with Billy's video game now find themselves handing the young Russian whatever he requests.

"I'll run it from the top," says Billy No-Beard, still sitting behind the controls. "If it doesn't stop blurring this time, I think we'll have to admit defeat."

"Never give up," mutters Mikhail. "Without street cams we can't make magic."

"I do realise how important they are for setting up tricks," replies Billy, sounding increasingly troubled by the situation, "but we can hardly complain to New Scotland Yard. If the police knew we'd patched into their traffic-monitoring system, I very much doubt they'd send a nice man round to fix the problem. We'd end up in care, or worse still with our *real* parents. Mikhail, it's been years since I felt the sting of my father's belt, and I'm never going back!"

Mikhail slides out now and sits up to face him. "Will you relax? Save the drama for the stage, huh? Even if we can't sort the problem right now, we'll find a way. I've reloaded the software, and that's fine – so it has to be the hardware. A loose connection, maybe, or a problem with the graphics card. I've checked everything, and even cleaned the fan, so I can't understand why it's still playing up." He turns, along with his two helpers, to look at the screen. The crowd shot on hold up there is zoomed in on the man in the mink with the dreamy trail behind him. "People just don't do that, after all, and the computer isn't wired for special effects."

"There has to be an explanation," says one boy, and glances nervously at his friend.

"Don't look at me," the other lad protests. "I came here to score goals. Instead I'm just spooked."

"OK, here we go." Billy taps softly at a key. In response, the footage begins to rewind. The crowds jitter backwards as expected, but the figure in the middle of the frame continues to confound them. He moves in reverse along with everyone else, but there's no stuttering with him. Instead, the man smoothly reabsorbs the blur he had created.

"I don't like the look of this one bit," mutters Mikhail. "The cameras capture one shot every ten seconds, but this guy is on film all the time. I just don't see how it's possible. As an illusion, it's impressive."

"It can't be an illusion," says Billy, still watching the slow-moving image. "If it was a trick, we'd know how to do it ourselves."

The two boys helping Mikhail face one another again. "I was joking when I said we were looking at a ghost," one squeaks, "but d'you think it could be for real?"

Billy stops the tape, and shares his look of concern. He clears his throat, attempts to say something, and then dismisses the idea completely. "Of course it isn't a *ghost*!" he declares, as if to convince himself. "Imagine if the new boy heard you talking like that? This is the freak of nature that chased Yoshi here in the first place, remember? It would scare him half to death to think he wasn't of this world."

"Billy's right," says Mikhail, toying nervously with the screwdriver in his hand. "But no matter what we think, perhaps we should put the boss in the picture."

*

Julius Grimaldi looks around the bank vault thoughtfully. He presses a finger to his chin, his snowy eyebrows seesawing as he considers one wall of deposit boxes then the next. "If I remember rightly, we won't have to go far to dig up the mute boy's pictures."

"You left them in *here*?" splutters Yoshi.

"Robbers emptied this place years ago," replies Julius, squinting to read the numbers on the boxes. "In many ways it's probably more secure now than it was under lock and key, because there's no reason for them to return." With that, his eyes zone in on a box across the vault. It isn't locked when he tests it, but the dust that falls away tells Yoshi that it hasn't been opened for some time. With great care, Julius lifts out a plastic tube. He pops the lid like a champagne cork, and looks quietly pleased when a roll of papers slips out intact.

"I was tempted to destroy these pictures at the time," he says, moving to flatten them out on the upturned safe. "The poor boy became distressed as soon as he put pen to paper," he adds. "What I never found out was where it had taken place, which is why I held onto them. Now, why don't your familiarise yourself with them, my boy? Tell me if the location seems familiar."

His curiosity fired, Yoshi peers over the first drawing. His first response is how sparse it is, just a series of pencil traces. His second impression is the haste in which it has been scribbled onto the page.

"It's a room," he says cautiously, in case he's missed something. "A room with very high ceilings, and a wonky chair."

"We're not looking at a work of art, Yoshi. It's a remote viewing. What you're looking at is a visualisation from a very special mind."

"All I'm saying is the legs aren't drawn straight."

"Just look at the picture underneath," sighs Julius, as if this is not the first time a crew member has poured scorn on his interests.

Yoshi does as he is told, sees the same roughly drawn room and chair, but this time with a figure in the seat. "Is it supposed to be him?" he asks, referring to the mute lad. "Whatever special gift he might've had, drawing faces certainly wasn't one of them."

"Remote viewers don't see themselves," says Julius. "Nor can they see into the future or the past. What they see are events as they occur. The distance might be no object, but sometimes they can feel as if they're right there at the scene – and that can be traumatic." He turns the picture to study it briefly. "The identity of the youth drawn here remains a mystery. Even if the boy had found his voice, he became way too disturbed to communicate with me as the drawings progressed." Julius taps a finger on the sheet of paper clearly blotted with old tears. "Keep going, Yoshi. There are more pictures to get through."

Yoshi turns to the next sheet, sees the same scene but with some big machinery sketched in behind the boy. He studies the pencil swoops and markings on these hulking great additions, and figures they must be dials and switches.

"Are they monitors of some sort?" he asks, to no reply. "They look like old monitors to me."

The sheet underneath shows the addition of a web of strings, or wires, running from the machines to a cap on the boy's head. "Is he in hospital?" asks Yoshi.

"He's certainly undergoing some kind of test," says Julius. "But this is no hospital."

"How can you be sure?"

"Keep going."

The next page includes what must be a doctor or technician. He's wearing a long coat and holding a clipboard in his stick hands. On the following page another figure joins him. This one is heavier-set than them both, with a circle for a body instead of a thin trunk. His features might be hastily drawn, but those tight eyes, broad brow and bald head are unmistakeable.

"That's him!" cries Yoshi. "The man in the mink!"

"Right there in the frame," agrees Julius, watching

Yoshi closely as he turns the page. In the picture underneath, the brute has reached for a switch on one of the machines. "You're nearly there," the old man assures him. "You might want to prepare yourself for the way this finishes."

Yoshi glances at Julius, concern gathering in his expression. Then, under the glow of the lamplight, he slowly peels away the sheet that covers the last one in the sequence.

15

FAR FROM IT

What Yoshi sees isn't just unexpected. It's so startling that he steps back to take it all in. Everything from the previous drawings is featured – from the kid in the hot seat and the surrounding machines to the doctor and the brute Yoshi knows so well. What is different is that this sketch has been obliterated by the mute boy's own hand.

Such is the violence with which the picture is scribbled out that in places the pencil has ripped through the paper.

"It looks like an explosion," breathes Yoshi.

"Indeed it does." Julius pauses there, and waits until he has the lad's full attention. "An explosion of the mind."

Yoshi examines the picture once again. This time he touches the obliterated sketch of the boy in the chair. *"An explosion of the mind,"* he repeats to himself, feeling strangely connected to the plight of both the subject of this remote viewing and the psychic artist himself. "Do the scribbles mean something happened when that brute flipped the switch?" he asks Julius.

"I had so many questions to ask the poor lad about this picture. Sadly, just drawing it upset him so acutely that I had to pull him away."

"So what do you think it means?"

"I was hoping you could answer that," replies Julius.

Yoshi turns to the storm of pencil strokes once more. He has to blink to focus this time, and shake his head to clear that weird static crackle now interfering with his thoughts. Doing his best to ignore it, he turns to the last page in front of him. There's nothing on it, however. Just a blank piece of paper . . . a white sheet that seems to trigger an overwhelming flash right there behind Yoshi's eyes.

"Oh!"

"What is it?" asks Julius, concerned by the way his young charge sits up sharply. He waves a hand in front of Yoshi's eyes. With no response, he grips the boy gently by the shoulders. "What do you see, my friend? It's happening, isn't it? Paint a picture in your mind for me."

"I see a room." Yoshi is aware of the old man's voice. Even so, he is consumed by the image forming in his mind's eye as the flare begins to fade. "I see the same chair. Some high-tech stuff, too: flat screens and keyboards. There are no dials and switches."

"The equipment has advanced," breathes Julius, struggling to contain his excitement. "It *must* be happening now!"

"I see people entering the room. Some are wearing lab coats, but a couple look more like businessmen, and there's . . . uh-oh."

"What?"

"Our friend in the mink," whispers Yoshi, scowling to himself now. "There's a girl with him. Long, dark hair. High fringe. Pale skin. Black dress. About my age, maybe a year older. Fourteen, perhaps. She has lots of bangles on her wrists and one heck of a frown on her face."

"Hey!" says Julius. "You're good. You may not remember much about your past, but I'd suggest you've done this many times before. There's no faulting your powers of description."

"He's leading her to the chair now," Yoshi continues, still speaking under his breath as if fearing he might be heard by them. "She's making a big deal about wearing the metal cap with all the wires, but it's in place now all the same. I don't like it, Julius. It seems so real."

"That's because it *is* real. You're experiencing a remote view of a scene that is actually taking place as we speak. But can you pinpoint the location?"

"Something is happening!" Yoshi stops him with one hand, and then closes his eyes quite suddenly. Lines of concentration tighten into his expression. "This girl," he breathes. "This can't be right! She seems to be . . . glowing!"

"Can you go into detail, Yoshi? Paint this picture for me."

"It's like a haze of light spreading out around her body."

"An aura," whispers Julius, nodding now. "What you are witnessing is a field of psychic energy. Such a phenomenon surrounds us all, although very few people can see it."

"Wow. I know I've lost my memory, but that's still news to me."

"Then you must be viewing one gifted girl if she's able to express her aura to the untrained eye. Yoshi, it seems you're not the only special child in town right now!"

"It's glowing purple and blue, like a bruise."

"Which would suggest she's not feeling particularly sunny right now." Julius paces around the boy, hands behind his back now, watching him all the time. "The colour is often believed to mirror a person's emotional state."

"I told you she looked cross," says Yoshi, his eyes still shut. Then he seems to start and grimace as if in pain. "Oh no," he says. "I have to put a stop to it.

Something is about to happen that's upsetting her. She's in real distress!"

"Yoshi, it may feel as if you're there, as if you're even feeling what she's going through, but it's an illusion. A psychic trick, if you like. Without knowing the location, there is nothing we can do."

"*Leave her alone!*" The boy's eyes snap open. For a second he looks totally lost, like someone who has just escaped a nightmare and found themselves bolt upright in bed. "Where are we now?" he asks breathlessly, and turns to look around.

"The vault," replies Julius, and tips his head. "Have you lost your memory again?"

"Far from it." The boy comes round full circle, a glint of determination in his eye. "Do you know what's above us, Julius?"

"I believe we must be in the banking district," he says, with a note of intrigue. "Threadneedle Street, at a guess."

"Can you see a big dome from there?"

"A dome? That'll be St Paul's Cathedral! The famous Sir Christopher Wren was the architect, though I must say the work of his lesser-known apprentice remains much overlooked by the general public. Sir Chris had little interest in astronomy, you see."

"So," says Yoshi hesitantly, aware that he's talking to a figure with a lifelong passion here. "Is that a 'yes'? Can you see the dome from Threadneedle Street?"

"Can't miss it!" declares Julius. "The crown of the dome looms large to the west of the banking district. In fact its shadow falls over many of the streets and courtyards at the end of each day. We're talking basic archeoastronomy." He pauses there, fiddles with the cuffs of his jacket. "This isn't about banking though, is it?"

"Not exactly." Yoshi touches his temples with his fingers, as if to soothe away the last of a headache. He frowns to himself, still picking over what he has just seen. "But there may be a saving in store," he adds, pacing the floor now.

Julius looks set to press for an explanation, only to curse when a series of loud, abrasive bleeps blare from inside his coat. "Do excuse me," he mutters, and begins to search his pockets. "Now where is the infernal thing? Whenever it goes off I feel like a slave to the modern age."

"Is that a phone?" asks Yoshi, wincing at the volume. "I've never heard such a ringtone."

Julius pulls a face, signalling his own displeasure, and then finds what he is looking for. "I tend to leave the cutting-edge technology to the younger generation," he says, revealing what at first looks like a large, black brick with buttons on it. "But my crew insist I carry something portable so they know where I am. They fear I might take a fall and need to call for their assistance." He extends a telescopic aerial, and then ponders which button to press. "It's entirely unnecessary, of course, but they will worry."

"Julius, that thing looks the same age as me!"

"Which is no time at all, in the big scheme of things." He shrugs, holding what must be one of the earliest mobile phones in history with both hands. "The only reason I agreed to use such a newfangled gadget is because it works underground, you see."

"I bet it does!" the boy declares, feeling charged up now his head has cleared. "Are you sure it's safe? If you can receive a signal down here, imagine how it must be scrambling your brain!"

"Nonsense, boy."

"I'm surprised *your* head isn't glowing," adds Yoshi, still haunted by his vision of the girl with the aura.

"I might not *enjoy* using state of the art gadgets," says Julius, and punches a button that stops the ringing, "but this has done me no harm." He hoists the phone to his ear, clearly struggling with such a weight. "Hello? Yes . . . you have? When was this? You should have sent for me immediately. We'll be right there!" He stabs at another button. When a second attempt to switch it off fails, he hands the whole thing to Yoshi.

"Who was it?" asks the boy, noting the lack of a caller display. He selects the only red button on the panel, feels this ancient model actually power down in his hands, but decides against teaching Julius how to use it correctly right now. All he can think about is the final reel of his remote view into that room . . . and the girl screaming in protest.

It had been a scream of frustration and despair, not pain. Yoshi felt certain of that. What he couldn't fathom was how the eerie light around her began to travel through the wires attached to that pan over her head. She had tried to climb out of the chair, prompting the man in the mink to restrain her. With his big hands on her shoulders she had thrown her head back like some trapped wild animal. It was then Yoshi had witnessed light pour from her eyes and mouth like torch beams. Shocked to the core, his mind's eye had fled from the scene – soaring through the ceiling and the building itself, up into a sky at twilight. When gravity appeared to take over, his view had switched back to look down upon a roof garden in the shadow of a great dome.

That was the impression Yoshi had returned with on accelerating to earth, through a seam of foliage, shrubs and soil, then roof tiles, joists, floors, foundations, clay and finally steel . . . to a vintage bank vault in which he had snapped open his eyes and come to his senses once again.

"Billy is on the Bridge," says Julius, unaware of the boy's thoughts. Yoshi finds the old man has rolled the papers back into the tube. He returns it to the deposit box and straightens up, looking set to move out. "They're having problems with the main monitor."

"And they called *you* to fix it?"

"Yoshi, the problem he described sounds most fascinating."

"There's something I need to tell you," says Yoshi, as Julius swishes to the other end of the vault.

"Tell me about it on the way," he calls back.

"But I—"

"No buts! I want to know *exactly* what you saw."

Julius climbs through the blast hole into the tunnel so painstakingly dug by thieves with millions in mind, and then stops because something isn't right. He's used to the boy lagging – as he had when they left the ghost station – but the silence is all wrong this time. Indeed, when he turns, Julius Grimaldi can only think that Yoshi has pulled off the kind of vanishing act that most street magicians take an age to perfect.

16

A HEAD FOR HEIGHTS

Many years earlier, a daring band of villains might have climbed this rope to freedom. Perhaps it had been dropped into place by a lookout on street level. He might have had more than just a sharp eye and a gift for sailors' knots. Maybe he was the brains behind the master plan. The one who had plotted this escape route, up through an old iron grate in the gutter outside the bank itself.

Whether these rogues actually made it, and where they were now, is of no concern to Yoshi. They could be lounging on a beach in Rio, or pressing their faces between the bars at Strangeways Prison. Like so much he has discovered down here, this cord from the underground realm has clearly gone unnoticed by the world above. Just moments earlier, swinging out over the abyss again, Yoshi had figured that the knot securing the rope to the grille up there would be so caked in grime it was as good as invisible to anyone passing overhead.

Pushing his way up, clamping the rope with his hands and knees, the boy holds out hope that it will take him to the top. The further he ventures, the less secure it seems, and there's still the height of a house to climb. A weak light falls through the grille, which is the focus for his attention. It's just enough to show his lifeline brushing back and forth across a band of broken piping. He could be the weight on a clock pendulum, the way each new footing causes the rope to swing and scrape. What troubles him, as he continues his ascent, is the way it also begins to feel kind of elastic.

"Don't fray on me!" he hisses, urging himself not to look down. The rope must have come closer to breaking every time Julius travelled to and from this subterranean shoreline. Had the old man known, maybe he would've followed the boy to the lip of the vault right now, and begged him to come down. The short hop to the lost river was one thing, daring to climb to the surface quite another. Despite the risks, however, Yoshi will not be persuaded back now. It's the visions of the girl that drive him onwards, not least the thought that she was be in such distress. He may not have been present to step in and help her at the time, but he couldn't just walk away now. If Yoshi really did have a special gift to see beyond the naked eye, this quest to rescue her would be his making.

Several times, this strange angel had hijacked the boy's senses. What each viewing failed to reveal was her whereabouts. The room she was in could've been anywhere, until in the last viewing Yoshi took off like a rocket, leaving him with the impression that he was overlooking the building that contained her. Wherever she was being held stood in the shadow of a great dome. Of this he was quite certain. When Julius had suggested that such a feature dominated the district skyline directly above the bank vault, Yoshi knew just what he had to do. There was no time, the way he had seen it, to wind their way back to the bunker and regroup. It even explained why his vision had been so clear, intense and haunting – she must be close by, and he would find her.

"I might have lost my mind," he grunts to himself, only for his next breath to be knocked from his chest on banging into the mossy brickwork, "just don't lose your nerve, old son."

Cursing his precarious situation once more, Yoshi finds the next knot with his foot. He hauls himself up by his hands, only to feel himself sinking by a couple of centimetres. He gasps, and waits for the rope to settle. When it does, just a sigh of relief is enough to trigger the twang of fibres. He can't look up now, let alone glance down. All he can do is squeeze his eyes tightly shut, and try not to make the rope swing. "Help," he pleads quietly, to nobody in particular. "*Help* me!" As if in response, and with an awful jerk, the rope drops another notch. Yoshi tucks in tight against the cord, sees his life underground flash brightly before his eyes . . . and when it fades he is back in the room again.

The doctors are gone in this viewing, as is the brute. Looking through this psychic window in his mind, Yoshi sees that even the machines have been wheeled away. All that remains is the girl in the chair. When he sets eyes on her this time that bruising haze around her warms to a lipstick pink. What happens next almost causes him to fall off the rope in surprise.

"*You're watching me again,*" she says, a note of playfulness in her voice, and looks to the upper corners of the room. "*I can sense it.*" She nods to herself now, and all the time her aura brightens. "*I knew you'd come back.*"

From his precarious perch the boy calls out, if only to appeal for her assistance, but she doesn't seem to hear. Yoshi hears his echo fall away, and struggles to hold back a sob.

"*Hey, you seem upset,*" she says next, focusing on nothing in particular.

Just for a moment, Yoshi breaks free from his terror, and registers what this must mean. He clings to the rope as tightly as he can. She might not be able to see or hear him, but she's tuned in to his emotions for sure.

"*Hold on,*" she says next, sounding very certain. "*Whatever is going on, you can do it. Just be strong, and have faith in yourself. If anyone can do it, Yoshi, it's you.*"

This time, Yoshi catches his breath for a very different reason. *She knows me? She knows my name. She must know who I am!*

"*You're the first person to have escaped from this place in years,*" she continues, "*Of course, they've all been looking for you, scouring the streets day and night. Aleister has sworn to bring you back, but you must've given him the slip or he would've found you by now. He's taking his fury out on us instead: more tests to tap our energies, along with all the pretence that it's for our own good of course — but we can handle it. You know how it is, and so does he. Together, if we put our minds to it, we can be a force to be reckoned with.*"

The boy listens with his eyes screwed tightly shut. All this information seems so new and yet so familiar. Just knowing that she's aware of his presence strengthens his grip on the rope. So, too, does the sound of another fibre failing. It even persuades him to let go with one hand, get a grip above, and continue to climb from this chasm.

"Whoever you are," he says out loud, his mind still burning with this image of the glowing girl, "I wish you could help me out of here."

She seems to consult her thoughts at this. As if to confirm that she understands, the peachy haze around her grows richer. *"Don't let me down, Yoshi. You said you'd come back for me. For all of us. When I see you next, I want to know exactly what happened, right from the moment you made it to the rooftops."*

"The rooftops?" Yoshi gulps at the thought, still willing himself to keep scaling the rope. "So now I'm supposed to have a head for heights?"

From way down below, the faint sound of a disturbance in the water reaches the boy's ears. It's a churning and a whiplash splash that leaves Yoshi clinging to every word of the psychic pep talk he's just heard. He has to keep going. Hanging around would make him little more than a drop-in snack for jaws that are likely to be waiting wide open for him. Yoshi may not be able to see where he is climbing, but the mesmerising connection with this girl is enough to guide him. Just then he sees the aura surrounding her darken considerably. A look of concern crosses her face. She turns to glance at a door, says only: *"Come quickly, Yoshi. We're in this together—"*

And then she is gone.

Everything Yoshi can see before his eyes flares white. When it fades, the only light he can see is right above him. There it is. The last of the day shining weakly through a grille that is almost within his reach.

"Yes!" he cries, and then follows with a *"Nooo!"* on seeing the state of the rope in between.

For Yoshi has reached the outcrop of broken piping, and there's barely a thread left where the rope has frayed. It might as well be dental floss, stuck between two decayed teeth. Gingerly, he stretches one hand high. His fingers find the rope above the fast-fraying section, which he grabs desperately as the final fibre gives way to his weight.

The rope beneath him snakes away. A terrible silence follows, before it coils into the water too far below for him to contemplate. Right now, with just one hand gripping what remains of the old cord, Yoshi's concern is totally focused on survival. Dangling there with both legs flailing, the boy wishes the crew had revealed the secret behind that levitation stunt they had performed for him. Instead, with nothing up his sleeves but straining arms, he hauls himself up the rope with all the strength that he can muster.

"You're nearly there," he grunts, wishing that vision might appear in his mind once more like some genie from a bottle. The girl's encouragement had saved him from freezing up and waiting to fall, but there's no blinding flash this time. No transportation out of here. Instead, the only thing facing Yoshi is the grate just over his head. Through it, he can see the last spread of sunshine over the winter sky, and gives thanks that it isn't raining. Making it this far has been tough enough without dealing with a deluge from the drains, though he has no intention of just hanging around for the weather to turn. Instead, using the broken pipe work for a foothold, Yoshi presses his shoulder to the grate and gives it several hefty shoves.

At this time, London's rush hour is almost over. The city is no longer gridlocked. Cars and buses move freely, while those workers who have finally left their offices think of little more than supper, a nice hot bath and bed. All wrapped up against the cold, they keep their heads down and focus on getting home by the fastest means possible. This is not a moment in the day when people look around at London, and marvel at the architecture. Take the financial district, at the end of a long day's trading. Here, the pavements could have turned to gold and even the bullion traders wouldn't notice.

Right now, the electric gates to one former banking institution slide apart. The place had closed in disgrace many years ago, following a legendary assault on a supposedly impenetrable vault. It is the riches of the present occupant that has restored the place to its former glory, so it's no surprise when a white limousine purrs out into the street.

The windows are tinted, suggesting someone very important is seated comfortably inside, but not a single commuter pays any attention. Indeed, the attitude of the passenger in the vehicle is much the same. The magnificent dome of St Paul's Cathedral might rise behind the rooftops, but the figure in the back seat is too busy brooding to notice.

He dips his bald head into the palm of one hand, the mink-lined sleeve of his coat falling back to reveal the colourful oriental tattoo of a snake on his forearm. Nothing seems to turn his tight blue eyes: not even a grate suddenly jumping from the gutter as the car prowls into Threadneedle Street. The chauffeur happens to catch sight of this unusual event, and monitors it from his rear view. He's even moved to adjust the mirror to frame the appearance of some strangely jubilant young vagabond. The kid hauls himself out by his hands and knees, and then faces up to the open sky like an old friend.

The chauffeur returns his attention to the road ahead, easing this luxury car on its way. The street kid he's just seen is of no concern to his passenger in the back. Whatever has been troubling Mister Aleister these last days, interrupting his thoughts could wind up losing him a plum job behind the wheel and very possibly his driving licence, too. For his boss moved in high circles, from police to politicians, priests and beyond. Sometimes those circles seemed so high, the driver muses to himself, it wouldn't surprise him if the devil himself had sent Mister Aleister up here to do business on his behalf.

17

THIS MAN IS NO GHOST

When Julius Grimaldi reaches the Bridge, he finds every member of the crew crammed inside. All of them are facing the big screen at the back, in silhouette to the shambling figure with the white mane of hair. He gives no more than a glance at the bizarre footage of the bald-headed brute from the market that morning. What concerns the old man is the air of silent tension among his young street magicians. It's as if they believe this sinister figure, caught on camera up there, might somehow conjure his way off the screen and into their world.

"I'm back," says Julius, but nobody turns to greet him. "Hello?"

He sighs, and concludes it's only natural that these young illusionists and tricksters might be dumbstruck by evidence of real *magick*. He considers the figure in the mink once more, apparently leaving his mark in time as he prowls through China-town, and wonders what spell a rogue master of the discipline might cast over Yoshi should he be first to track him down.

On discovering his young charge gone from the bank vault, Julius had simply turned and retraced his steps back here. Any attempt to follow Yoshi on foot seemed futile. Julius was in the winter of his years, after all. The boy was more agile, and possibly more daring, than the old man could ever hope to be. Wherever the lad had taken himself, he would just have to go there alone. Besides, with what Julius had learned from Billy's call, Yoshi's destination might just be located on screen before the boy even arrived at it.

Charged up by the plan he intends to share with the crew, Julius clears his throat and says: "Would everyone face me!" He claps his hands, in vain it seems, for nobody turns from the on-screen action.

Julius sighs deeply to himself, and spots Billy at the controls. There he is, running the tape in slow motion until the moment the brute seemingly melts out of the market. At that point Billy stops, and winds back through the same sequence as if someone might spot how it's done.

"My guess is it's a spirit of some sort," the Executive Deck Hand says out loud, oblivious to the old man at the back, just like everyone else. "We're looking at Chinatown here, after all. I've heard Mae Ling say that opium vampires haunt the neighbourhood passageways. According to her, those blood-freaks often surface from their smoking dens to haunt the alleyways in search of fresh prey."

"Really?" pipes up one small boy, looking very pale all of a sudden.

"So he *is* a spectre," says one of Billy's wingmen from across the floor. "I knew it as soon as I set eyes on him."

"Once they've sucked the life out of their victims," continues Billy solemnly, "they bleed them dry of money and score the drugs they need to sedate themselves again. A horde of opium vampires has haunted this quarter for well over a hundred years, apparently. Ever since the community was founded, according to Mae Ling. If Yoshi is his next victim, maybe we'll be next. He might pick *us* off, one by one."

"Don't spook me!" squeaks the kid. "I haven't been frightened for years."

"It isn't a ghost or an opium vampire." This is Mikhail, addressing everyone crossly. "It's a myth. An unpleasant kind that's often cooked up when immigrants settle, and I should know. I am proud to be from Russia, but that does not mean I have ever worn a fur hat and danced like a Cossack! Even stupid people accept that once they get to know me, and quit demonising me for being different from them."

"But I heard the story from Mae Ling!" protests Billy sheepishly.

"Like so many of these tall stories," Mikhail tells him, "it's become part of Chinatown's folklore. The residents here might be a superstitious sort, but since when did we buy into anything that has no explanation, huh?"

"So if he isn't a drug-addicted Dracula then explain what's happening here!" Billy jabs a finger at the big screen, and rewinds the sequence once again. "Does *anyone* have any answers?"

The hush that follows is even thicker than the silence in which Julius had found them. He steps back to the door to take it all in. Never has he witnessed a crew seem so unsure of themselves. He finds himself reflecting on all those generations of runaways and street children who have found their feet here over the years. Across the surface of this city – he consoles himself with a note of pride – a small but growing band of adults are making the most of their lives, thanks to the chance this bunker offered them. Sure, a few continue to perform illusions on the streets. Indeed, one individual has even made it as a celebrity mind manipulator. Even those who pursue careers in everything from air traffic control to zoology still stow the odd trick up their sleeve. A little juggling of incoming aircraft could help avoid disaster, as could misdirection when entering the lions' den to remove a thorn from a paw. Whatever walk of life they now tread, however, every single individual remains united in wanting to keep this bunker the best-kept secret in town. There is nothing to hide in this old tin can, admits Julius to himself, but peeling away the lid would expose too many vulnerable souls to the miserable existence they've each escaped.

For a kid like Yoshi, it didn't just place him in danger, but could threaten all London as well. Having seen the child's potential, and with his memory of the mute boy's powers fresh in his mind once more, Julius considers his crew and wonders if any more gifted individuals exist within this city.

The old man twiddles his fingers as he thinks. He goes through the times he has tried and failed to tap into the energy whizzing around the Faerie Ring. Yoshi may not have restored the power with one touch. Then again, the poor lad appeared to have lost all memory of his gift. Maybe it would come to him in time, decides Julius, and remembers briefly that he has returned to the Bridge in order to retrieve him. Having lost one poor soul with the same extraordinary gift, all those years ago, he is not going to fail Yoshi in the same way.

"May I *please* have your attention," he asks, with a hint of exasperation, only to fall as quiet as his crew. For a thought catches up with him that brightens his eyes. His restless fingers fall still, struck now by a solution to the conundrum that has consumed so many of his years. Then he begins to count, his digits uncurling one at a time: a full hand on his left side, one finger and thumb on the other.

"Seven!" he declares under his breath, thinking of the times this sacred number has featured as part of the puzzle. "To master the ring, there have to be *seven* individuals who share the same gift as Yoshi."

Looking at it like this made the solution seem so simple. Firstly there had been the plate on his dog tag with the numerical sequence stamped onto it. Then there was the Seven Dials, the name of the monument where Julius had introduced Yoshi to the mystery at the heart of his life's work. This self-styled archeoastronomer and psychogeographer had shown him some breathtaking patterns that appeared to bind this city to some kind of cosmic order: the seven stars in the sky, the seven steeples aligned to them, and finally one of seven waypoints underneath each church, connecting seven ley lines in the Faerie Ring. Altogether, this amounted to just six elements. The seventh element was the seven gifted souls. So in accordance with the pattern, Yoshi alone was not enough. He might be tuned into the energies encircling the city, but recharging them demanded seven pairs of hands – not one. With all of them trained to connect with a waypoint properly – why, the energy they might conjure between them could protect the city for centuries! Alternatively, they could open up London to the very worst of all possible futures. That, he thinks to himself, depends on who brings them together.

"Oh dear," whispers Julius, and carries his gaze from floor to screen.

This time, he sees the figure up there in a very different light. The trail behind him is of no interest. He knew what was causing it straight away. After all, cameras often captured auras in people who possessed psychic abilities. The nature of the haze depended on the level of their gift, of course. In very rare cases, such a mist of psychic energy is forceful enough to be seen with the naked eye, but Julius has never encountered an individual in possession of such powers. Even if the crew believed him, now is not the time for a lesson in earth magick. *This brute is clearly in pursuit of a similar goal*, thinks Julius. As soon as Yoshi had identified him from the sketches drawn by the mute boy, he suspected they shared an interest in mining the same hidden seams of superhuman ability. Judging by the way the man had menaced both kids, however, it was likely their intentions for the ring couldn't be more different. What alarms the old man is the fact that Yoshi is no longer under his wing. This figure captured by the street cameras had clearly returned to Chinatown to track him down. *Heaven help us all*, he thinks to himself, considering the worst that could happen should the brute catch up with his quarry.

Mindful of the challenge they face in clawing the boy back to their fold, Julius brings his hands together with a commanding clap.

"This man is no ghost!" he announces, and is delighted to see everyone turn as if he's only just swept in. "But his existence could haunt us for a long time unless we act *now*. Yoshi is at large somewhere. But your so-called spectre is not out to haunt him. Oh, no. He's out to *hunt* him. If we fail to get to Yoshi first this bunker could be history for a second time – in a city quite literally on the rocks."

"So what can we do?" asks Mikhail.

"Start by forgetting about the trail he's left behind for the camera." Julius strides onto the Bridge with a purpose now, parting the crew as he speaks. "There is a simple explanation, but none of you will accept it until you learn to be more like your audience, and suspend your disbelief. Right now, what matters doesn't lie behind this fur-lined hulk. Forget about this blur, or whatever you want to call it. For Yoshi's sake, we need to discover where he was heading!" The last of the crew move to one side as he briefs them, revealing Billy at the controls. "Can you do that?" asks Julius, resting his hands on the back of the boy's chair.

The Executive Deck Hand sucks the air between his teeth. "Can *I* do that?" He cracks his knuckles noisily. It's a show of confidence that had been badly lacking just a moment earlier. "I could've tracked Yoshi down hours ago if this sorry bunch hadn't spooked themselves so badly. Honestly, you should have heard some of the suggestions. It was embarrassing!"

"I did," Julius leans over Billy to find one crimson ear, "and it was."

18

SECOND NATURE

Out in the open at last, the first thing Yoshi notices are the cameras. He climbs from the open grate, brushes himself down, and is struck by how many he can see. There are traffic cameras on every junction and street corner, and surveillance cameras mounted over office doors and gates, just like those closing behind him.

Yoshi had caught just a glimpse of the white limousine as it swept past. Unlike the boy, the vehicle had been spotless and gleaming. He might not remember much about this city, but this makes him think it was kind of carved up and divided. There were those at the top, with the finest views and luxuries. Then there were those below. Some stretching so far down it was doubtful that the rich and powerful even knew of their existence.

"OK," he says to himself, feeling the cold out here. "Let's go to work."

A girl contained in a building. A prison, perhaps,

in the shadow of a dome. With this information in mind, Yoshi steps away from the gate, circling to find his bearings. Businessmen with brollies and briefcases steer around him, barely noticing this kid with the grimy face and clothes. Even the evening traffic is light enough for him to drift across the road with his eyes on the skyline.

But the dome is nowhere in sight. From ground level, all Yoshi can see are the imposing stone buildings that flank the street, and the early stars twinkling in the strip of sky above. There's nothing of note here but gated courtyards, stone pillars and steps leading up to dour-looking doors. If these are banks and money markets, the boy thinks to himself, they don't seem very welcoming. Then again, he decides, maybe that's the idea. Yoshi hugs himself to keep warm, wishing the world would turn white for a moment, and a vision appear to guide him. There are more pedestrians on this side of the street, heading for a tube station at the far end. A small part of him feels like joining them, heading for the warmth and certainty on offer underground, but this girl and her plight continue to haunt him. He steps back, away from the path of people, and leans against the lower rungs of a fire escape.

"Where now?" he says to himself, thinking what he really needs is an earpiece and a direct line to the

Bridge. At least then he could receive directions. He looks up at a nearby traffic camera, and then lets his shoulders sag. With a thousand and one views of this city, there's no chance the crew would be observing this very street right now. What is there to draw them to this one, after all?

Just then, a woman wrapped up for winter walks by. She's led by three toy poodles on leashes. One of the dogs seems interested in the boy, causing the woman to halt. It sniffs at Yoshi's feet, growls when the boy dips down to pet it, and then cocks one leg just to finish the insult.

"Hey!" cries Yoshi, jumping away just in time. The woman scowls at him, as if the dog has every right to use a street kid like him as a pee-post, and then tugs the poodles onwards with her nose high in the air. Yoshi watches her go. He rests his hand on a rung, shaking his head at such snobbery and rudeness. At the far end of the street, the entrance to the underground station looks more inviting than ever.

What comes to mind next doesn't feature a bright flash or a vision, but prompts him to grip the ladder's cold rung tightly.

On the street, thinks Yoshi, things just can't get much worse. Which means the only way from here, of course, is *up*!

The fire escape covers four storeys. At the very

top, Yoshi crawls over the parapet, and rolls onto his back for a moment. On scaling past the first window, he had felt a shiver drop down his spine. It was one that had suggested it may not be a good idea for him to look down. By the third window, that shiver had spread and turned to outright terror. His fear of falling had been bad enough in the abyss below ground. Out here, he could actually see how far he had to drop. And yet, despite it all, Yoshi claws his way to the top. The sense of peril that might paralyse some was not going to hold him back here. If anything, it leaves him feeling quite alive. At the summit, facing up to the evening sky, Yoshi realises his heart is hammering from the *thrill* of it all as much as the fear. Gazing at the wheel of stars, it feels almost second nature to be this far from the ground.

Sitting up on his elbows now, Yoshi takes stock of his new, elevated position. What he sees lights up his face in more ways than one. There it is, beyond the air-conditioning units, weather vanes and water tanks – the one thing he's been hoping to see. With the last of the sunshine setting in the background, the dome of St Paul's has an aura all of its own. The boy stares at it long enough for this crescent of light to turn from honey to bronze. It's such a magnificent view that he has to remind himself why he's here. Standing now, he regards his new surroundings, and everything seems so much clearer.

"There it is," he says out loud. His eyes narrow, fixed as they are on a building tucked away behind this imposing terrace. It's the one he hopes and prays contains the girl he had seen in his mind's eye. The location certainly fits in with the one he had viewed remotely. As does the lush greenery spilling over the upper tiles, for he had certainly passed through such a layer on his imaginary rise and fall through the building. "The roof garden!"

It looks like a little square of rainforest, such is the effect of the bamboo, fern and pampas grass that have been cultivated over there. This time, Yoshi's heart starts pumping at the prospect of getting inside. Whatever is going on within those walls, he has to see it with his own eyes. The eye in his mind might have led him to this point, but it hadn't flashed open on the climb. If anything, it leaves the boy feeling like he's on his own from here. He knows where he's supposed to go. The problem is reaching it. Yoshi takes himself to the far side of the roof, and studies the gap between the parapet and the building in question. You could fit a bus in there, he thinks. Lengthways.

"I can't jump that far," he mutters. "Can I?"

From this vantage, it's clear that such a gap surrounds the entire building. The space below looks immaculately landscaped, with paths and benches, and a snaking water feature with orange segments floating in it that the boy decides must be koi carp. Whoever works here, he thinks, clearly has plenty of perks. It certainly looks like a great deal has been invested in the place. The stonework has been recently cleaned, and the balconies finished with a fresh lick of black, gloss paint. Only one thing stops the boy from heading back down to the street and finding his way in on foot, and that's the guards. He can see half a dozen at least, prowling the paths, smoking cigarettes in doorways, and several keeping watch at the courtyard entrance. Are these goons here to prevent intruders getting in, thinks Yoshi, crouching now at the edge, or to prevent people from leaving?

Either way, he decides, there's only one way to find out. Yoshi sizes up the distance one more time, only to sigh with frustration. It's no good. Just thinking about attempting such a leap leaves him giddy. He moves away from the edge, turns and sits with his head in his hands.

"What can I do?" he says out loud. "I'm not brave enough."

"You can do it, Yoshi." The voice floats out of nowhere. He looks up with a start, but there's nobody there. Just a few pigeons squabbling for space on a television aerial. *"I knew you'd come again."*

161

The girl. It had to be. The weird one with the fringe and the scowl, not to mention that freaky glow like the sun was permanently behind her.

"Where are you?" he says, up on his feet now. "Can you see me?"

"No," the voice replies, upon which that familiar flare sears into his vision . . . and there she is once more. Looking to the upper corners of the room she's in, with a faint but certain smile. *"I can't see you, Yoshi. But I sense that you can see me."*

Still standing close to the edge, but blind to his surroundings, the boy grins to himself. "I'm close," he says, viewing her clearly in his mind again, "but not close enough."

He sees her tip her head to one side. The glow around her brightens once more. *"I wish you were here,"* she says. *"All I can do is sense your presence, but something tells me there's a problem. You're close, I can feel it, and yet you might as well be a million miles away. That's what I'm picking up from you."*

"I'm on the roof of the building," says Yoshi, aware now that she can't hear him, but speaking his mind in the hope that it helps. "The gap is too far for me to jump. What do you suggest?"

She doesn't respond. Just keeps on switching her gaze between imaginary points in the room. Yoshi shifts his weight from one leg to the other, waiting for her to direct him. He sees her stand now, as if in greeting, and that's when the vision turns white once more.

"Nothing can hold you back, Yoshi. The way you escaped pretty much defied the laws of gravity. Wherever you are, I have every faith that you can make it back again."

The flash fades with her voice. Yoshi blinks, his eyes smarting. When his focus returns, he finds himself looking down at his feet. It takes a moment for him to realise that he's perched on the lip of the building by his heels, and steps back with his heart in his mouth.

"Ohmygoodness!" he cries, windmilling his arms for balance. Despite the shock, he doesn't back off any further. The drop might be deadly, but something tells him he's been here before. That prickling sensation is back again, along with a giddy kind of thrill. Altogether, it makes him feel, well ... *complete*. It's as if this kind of acrobatic stunt is something he's pulled off in the past. He levels his gaze across the divide, thinking back to what the girl had said about the nature of his escape. Yoshi may not recall what he was doing in this building, but to seemingly defy gravity meant only one thing – he must have fled via the rooftops. And if he'd made it to the aerial garden over there, somehow he would've had to cross this same divide.

Acting on impulse now, Yoshi steps forward.

As the path and the pond appear below, he feels like he's about to go into a somersault, especially when the ball of one foot finds nothing underneath. Carefully, he returns one heel to the edge of the parapet, followed by the other. There, he takes a deep breath and stands to attention, seeking to find both calm and balance.

Across from this lone figure on the skyline, beyond the drop before him and the roof garden opposite, a faint glimmer of light remains over the dome of St Paul's Cathedral. Without it, this central London landmark, designed by the great architect Sir Christopher Wren, would be shrouded in darkness. Elsewhere around the city, sensing darkness approach, floodlights fire up to illuminate a jagged ring of churches constructed by Sir Christopher's apprentice – a mysterious young visionary by the name of Nicholas Hawksmoor.

Feeling strangely calm, Yoshi steps away from the ledge. He turns, takes ten paces across the roof, then comes around to face the dome again. And there, with the cycle from day to night complete, he prepares to test his strange angel's belief in him. With his sights locked on the far ledge, softened with ivy and palm fronds, the boy sprints for the abyss.

19
WITHOUT WINGS

With every footfall, Yoshi feels closer to his former
life. His calf muscles work like pistons, and a sense
of determination and poise flow through him. It's
a charge that keeps him focused, stops him from
pulling up. *I have done this before*, he tells himself.
This is not going to be a big mistake . . .

The edge of the building rushes up so quickly that
it feels like the roof is being whipped away from
under his feet. He lengthens his final stride, keeps
his head high and springs from the parapet with all
his might.

Should a guard in the gardens below chance to
look up at this moment, they'd see stars filling the
void between the two buildings. If this was enough
to capture their imagination, they'd be rewarded
by another breathtaking sight – a boy without wings
in flight. At first his arms and legs are behind
him, but midway through this brave leap he swings
them forward. From ground level, had any of them

actually noticed, such a stunt might seem perfectly executed. For the boy disappears from sight just as abruptly as he had appeared.

Yoshi doesn't arrive in this rooftop rainforest with the same grace and ambition that accompanied his launch. In fact, he crashes into the undergrowth as if a slingshot has hurled him there. All the foliage serves to soften his landing, however, as well as swallow him completely. When he surfaces, spitting out soil and picking twigs from his hair, it takes a second for him to realise just what he's achieved.

The boy looks at the building he's left behind, and senses with absolute conviction that he escaped from here the way he just arrived. He reaches for the fading bump on his head, aware now why it had seemed so odd to him that he should suffer so much from what he'd thought was such a basic fall. Then there had been his interest in the upper levels of this city, and not just when Julius had let the moonlight flood inside the summit of the Seven Dials. Even Mikhail had noticed him checking out the rooftops from the alley. He'd even spelled it out to him.

"I'm a free runner," says Yoshi to himself. This morning, those words hadn't rung any bells. Now they pealed away inside his mind. "I'm a *parkour!*" The way this last term leaves his lips, it doesn't sound foreign at all. Nor does he feel any need to translate it to himself, for he knows full well what it means.

Rising to his feet on this verdant rooftop, a string of memories spool through Yoshi's mind – of moonlit jumps, high-wire twists and rooftop vaults he'd been forced to perform in a desperate bid for freedom. They play out like a show reel, reminding the boy how he'd crossed London without once touching the ground. As a parkour, it wasn't the first time he'd travelled in this way. A parkour took a map, and drew a long, straight line from A to B without a care for the layout of the streets. Whatever obstacles the line crossed, from multi-storey car parks to housing estates laid out like dominoes, a parkour would find a way over and around them. Why stick to pavements? That's what a true disciple would ask, as Yoshi recalls so clearly now. A parkour didn't need a skateboard or a mountain bike to make the most of this city land-scape. Just a boundless imagination, physical grace, and an ability to flow like water no matter what stood in your way. It wasn't a gift, like the one Julius had been so keen to explore with him. This ability, Yoshi can say with absolute certainty, he has mastered from scratch. Aware now that he is standing on top of a building he has been inside before, the mist that masks all memory of his escape continues to clear. Indeed, as he recalls now, the city itself had been quite fog-bound several nights earlier ... when he called upon his flair as a free runner to escape with his life.

"Oh my," Yoshi whistles to himself, reflecting on how his flight out of here had enraged his pursuer. Too bulky to scale the heights after him, the brute had shadowed the boy from below, threatening him with a sticky end if he didn't come down right away. But Yoshi had ignored him, and continued to leap and bound over the lamplit streets, scrambling from one building to the next.

By the time he had arrived over London's theatreland, poor Yoshi was on his last legs. He had kept to one side of Shaftesbury Avenue, hopping, swinging, reaching and jumping his way between pitched roofs, glass domes and oversized hoardings for musicals and shows. If only he hadn't been tempted to stop to catch his breath on the huge electronic billboard overlooking Piccadilly Circus, he might have lost his pursuer on the pavement way below. At the time, it really seemed to Yoshi that he'd pulled it off. There he was, perched on the lower gantry of the massive advertising screen, thankful that the only thing showing at that time of night was a sponsor's logo set against a thick black frame. Among the late revellers, he had spied a familiar bald dome turning circles on the spot. There he was, below the statue of Eros, the god of love – although there was none lost between these two. It had amused the boy to watch him scour this busy intersection, helpless after all this time. Yoshi would've happily stayed on his perch until the brute had abandoned his search, had his back not suddenly heated up as millions of tiny lamps burst into light.

As an advertisement for himself, Yoshi couldn't have made a bigger impact. Even the flashy sequence that fired up behind him had never drawn such an audience. First, the boy's presence earned a shriek from the far pavement, and then hands shot up to point at him. Cast in silhouette by the giant LED screen, the boy found himself the centre of attention for more than just the man in a mink. With no time to plan properly, he had dropped from the ledge onto the roof of a slow-moving doubledecker bus – and pulled off the stunt to perfection!

Except that the bus promptly halted at a passenger stop. What's more, the man who then muscled his way to the front of the queue didn't look like he was hoping to find a quiet seat for a snooze. Unwilling to hang around for the brute to snatch him from the roof, Yoshi had been left with no choice but to break the number one free runner's rule.

He had dropped to the ground, and fled on foot.

There, the chase had really kicked in. With no height or acrobatic advantage over the brute, Yoshi had been forced to hit the streets as fast as his legs would carry him. He possessed the speed and stamina to outrun the man. What let the boy down was London at street level. It just wasn't a familiar environment to him, unlike the gables and parapets above. By the time Yoshi had blundered into the veils of fog over Chinatown, the gap was beginning to close. Had the boy not gone to earth in a dead-end alley, he wouldn't be right here now on this rooftop garden. Where the story of his escape had started.

20

FROM THE TOP DOWN

Turning to face the foliage, Yoshi doesn't just feel revived. The return of at least some of his memory makes him feel *reborn*! The vision thing may have set him apart from most other kids, but his ability to free run lifted him way over their heads. Still, he reminds himself, it hadn't quite secured his freedom that night of the chase. If anything, it had dropped him into a world that was both thrilling and chilling in equal measure. Yoshi thinks of the crew of tricksters and illusionists he has left behind, and the old man who showed him the magic that both encompassed the city and defied all explanation. He feels bad, just turning his back on them, but this is a personal matter he has to sort out himself. Even so, Yoshi can't help thinking he would feel a whole lot less nervous if that band of young street performers was behind him right now.

Across the roof garden, up-lights have been planted in the soil. Shadows sway among the palm fronds, which bow as the boy wades in like some Victorian explorer of old. Blades of pampas grass close behind the path he forges, as if drawing him in deeper. Just as Yoshi begins to worry about the size of the venus fly-traps he's had to step around, he pushes out into a clearing. At the centre, sunk into the roof, is a big skylight. The way it glows so brightly reminds the boy of campfires, but from a time he can't recall. Even so, with his past beginning to spark and crackle again, Yoshi hopes it won't be long before the story of his life burns bright as a beacon. Creeping out of the undergrowth, careful not to make a sound, Yoshi dares to peek through the glass.

What he sees takes him back, but to where, remains a mystery. The skylight overlooks a central space all the way down to another exotic landscape in the lobby. The centrepiece is a folly of the highest order: some kind of tropical water feature, finished with mangrove and ringed by boulders chiselled into benches. A number of hallways lead into this central area, reminding the boy of spokes in a bicycle wheel.

Several floors are stacked around this atrium, with polished marble surfaces and balconies bearded by hanging plants. None of it brings any memories to mind, but Yoshi has been to this place before, without a doubt. And spent quite some time here, too, if his sense of recognition is to be believed. What concerns him more than anything is the presence of so many guards. Even on the upper level, he can see several leaning against the balcony, admiring the miniature Eden below. It's an impressive layout, he has to admit. Yoshi even begins to wonder whether anything bad could occur in a place like this. He had half expected to find some grim interrogation centre with wire cages and manacles. This looks more like a private hospital . . . or a research foundation, perhaps, set up by an investment bank looking to profit from the future.

The thought hangs over Yoshi like a bulb with a broken filament. It doesn't shed light on what he's looking at here. It just *feels* as if it would do if everything was working properly in his mind. Bit by bit his memory continues to come back. It's as if this vision thing of his had encouraged him here, knowing it would jog yet more recollections. If he really was in possession of a psychic power, a knock to the head clearly couldn't touch it. And with so much more to discover about himself, he decides, this place right under his nose could prove to be as familiar to him as the lifelines on the palm of his hands.

Yoshi rests his chin on his fists, lost in thought. The view from here is really quite pleasant, he decides, as is the jungle surrounding him. So when a young girl's angry shout shatters the peace, Yoshi is up on his hands and knees, ready to fight or take flight. Another cry, this time from a guard, who rushes around the balcony on the middle floor towards the source of the outburst. His call for assistance echoes across the atrium, as does the squeak of jackboots on marble. At the same time, a bright glow spreads out to the balcony, out of which backs a woman in a white coat with her hair up in a bun. Despite his bird's-eye view, Yoshi can't quite see what's causing this intense display. Even so, he's forced to squint as the glare turns a seething shade of scarlet, and then gasps as a plate and a flurry of sandwich squares fly out from the same source.

"I will not eat!" shouts a voice. *"Not until you stop punishing us just because Yoshi was smart enough to escape!"*

"Do stop saying he escaped," the woman replies. She may have managed to sidestep the plate, but the calm in the tone of her voice can't disguise her annoyance. "Everyone here is admitted by consent of their families, as you know very well."

"So why do these goons lock our doors at night?"

"To keep you safe from yourselves," she answers firmly. By now, the guards have arrived on the scene. Even so, they keep their distance, gathered as they are on the fringe of this hot-looking haze. "It's all part of the treatment."

174

"Treatment?" the girl sounds like she's paused to spit her contempt on the floor. *"Don't insult me!"*

"Your parents are aware of our techniques. If they harboured any doubts they would never have released you into our care for the duration of the programme."

"So why can't I just call them, huh?"

"Because, Livia, they have appointed us to be your temporary guardians. They recognise that complete immersion in the programme is required for you to make a full recovery, which means no contact with the outside world. Like us, they don't want you to feel ashamed or persecuted for the special things that you can do. We're here to help you connect with your inner self, so that ultimately we're able to release you in full control of your capabilities."

Yoshi listens intently, watching the guards out by the balcony trade glances like the girl is totally cuckoo. He notices the wash of light has ebbed from their feet, like a slow tide on the turn.

"I don't want to *control* my aura!" he hears the girl say, sounding quieter but still as spiky, "It's a part of who I am, and you lot can't control me!"

"You need to remind yourself why you're here, Livia. Even you must admit that what sets you apart from others has caused you grief and persecution." The woman in the white coat stands her ground. The glare she's facing continues to retreat, stopping in front of her shoes now. "You may feel cut off from the world around you right now, but you're not isolated from those who have been through a similar experience. Together with the other residents you can make sense of it, and be stronger as a result."

"We're freaks," the girl called Livia replies plainly. *"Why don't you just say it to my face? We've all heard the staff here talk about us like we belong in a circus sideshow."*

The woman sighs. "You're not freaks. You simply have minds that appear to work on a unique level."

"So we're freaks."

"Livia, you have to eat. Without food you'll grow weak."

"Which means I'll be useless to the Foundation. You'd have to find another guinea pig to take my place for Aleister's experiments, and that would be a setback, wouldn't it? In fact, with Yoshi gone, you'll have to make that two!"

As the girl voices her irritation, so the glow begins to build once more. The guards shift away, looking a little restless now. The woman in the white coat retreats by a step, showing her palms to the source of the light now.

"Oh, Livia. Please stop testing my patience," she says, with some hesitation this time. "Aleister is a therapist, as well you know. In bringing so many of

you together, he simply wants everyone on the programme to feel united. It's not an experiment. It's a
healing process. The sense of harmony is intended to
restore your self-confidence. Ultimately, it'll help
you to control your . . . *special nature.*"

The way she says this makes Yoshi smile, for it's
plain the woman doesn't wish to stir up the livid
haze coming from this unseen girl. He clasps his
hands under his chin, almost enjoying the light
show below.

"If this is a group project," the girl can be heard to
say next, *"why does he pay so much attention to just a
few of us?"*

"Livia, your welfare is our priority. Everything
from the gardens to the games room is designed to
bring out the best in everyone. Aleister's approach
is to provide select groups quality time. You're
one of the lucky few. If everyone went on his city
excursions, you wouldn't enjoy the benefit of his
personal coaching."

"Oh, let's not start on the day trips," Livia complains. *"I don't want to visit another church until I'm
carried inside one in a coffin."*

"Education and enlightenment is all part of the
programme."

"But it's so boring!" the girl complains, and the
haze pulses around the woman in the white coat.
"I'm not interested in architecture or history. Besides, as

soon as we get there Aleister spends most of his time on a mobile phone."

"You're not the only one who deserves a trip, madam. There are seven church excursions for him to orchestrate so that every member of your group can share the same experience independently."

"But why can't we just go to the cinema?"

"That's enough!" The woman in the white coat jabs her hands to her hips. It's clear to Yoshi that she's lost all patience, for she doesn't flinch when the glare surrounding her begins to flex and flash. "You're setting a bad example to everyone else, and we will not tolerate it! Now, eat your supper, brush your teeth, get to bed and switch off your lights. Communicating with you, Livia, is like trying to hold down a conversation in a cheap disco!"

The silence that greets the woman's outburst weighs heavier by the second. Yoshi senses that all is not well, as do the guards down there. They back away from the light as it pools once more, and then freeze when it swirls and eddies around the woman.

"I'll eat if that's what you want," the girl announces, sounding deeply fed up. *"Just let me dine in peace!"*

At first Yoshi thinks he is witnessing yet another levitation trick. For this stern-looking woman suddenly drops her hands from her waist and appears to rise up off the floor. From his vantage point, it looks like she's on tiptoe, but then the balls of her feet lift away too. Horrified, she looks to her toes, then appeals to the girl for release.

"Put me down!" she shrieks. "I will not tolerate this level of insolence!"

"*Too late*," the girl replies, chuckling as the object of her scorn floats up and away, over the heads of the astonished-looking guards, and out into the atrium.

"Stop this!" Kicking her legs in vain, the woman shrieks in frustration as one shoe slips away. It drops two flights, splashing into the water feature below, followed by the woman herself. She doesn't fall so fast, however, but seems to descend quite gently in the clutches of this swirling light. She thrashes and curses and protests all the way, pausing only for a shocked intake of breath on receiving the dowsing Yoshi believes she deserves. For a moment, she disappears under the murky surface of the water. When she returns, her neat hair is so coated in weed she could be sporting dreadlocks. Yoshi doesn't stop to see her climb out, or wait for the final trade of insults. For what he has just witnessed both amazes him and makes perfect sense. As the guards rush down to haul the woman onto the rocks, he tests the skylight seal with his fingers. Yoshi pulls at it until a quiet cracking sound tells him that he's in. He may not recall vowing to this girl that he would return, but abandoning her now is out of the question. Coming to her rescue is something he feels like he has to do. Judging by the episode he's just witnessed, clearly only a fool would dare to get in Livia's bad books.

21

ONE SUGAR OR TWO?

Warm air rises from the atrium to greet Yoshi. With his fingertips under the seal now, he lifts and then shifts the skylight to one side. If he drops down from here, the pond in the lobby won't cushion his fall. A free runner might know how to absorb the bone-shattering shocks from all kind of leaps, but they also had to respect their limits. Yoshi bites his lower lip. It's one thing to have rediscovered his calling as a parkour. For the sheer rush, it even beats this psychic eye of his. All he needs to recall now is just how far he can go with each gift.

"Tell me, Livia, when will you learn some respect for authority?" Way below, despite submitting to the care of the guards, the soaking wet woman continues to rant and rage. She glowers at the floor from which she's just been so breathtakingly evicted, though the misty light has retracted now. In fact, Yoshi can't decide if it's an aura or the glare from a fluorescent strip coming through an open door. "Even if you'd earned another day trip," shouts the woman from below, her sense of duty gone, "you've blown it now. I'm ordering the door to your quarters to be locked, for the safety of my staff, do you hear? One day's confinement should encourage you to realise that abusing your powers like that is wholly unacceptable!"

"Abusing my *powers?"* comes the astonished reply, from the girl who Yoshi has yet to see. *"Our parents think you're helping us get to grips with our abilities. They have no idea that you treat us like laboratory animals. Now* that *is what I call an abuse of power!"*

A guard stands on the upper level. He's leaning against the balcony, looking quietly amused by this exchange of insults. He watches the woman being led from the lobby. Man, he's seen some crazy things within these walls. Witnessing the doctor being dumped from a great height wasn't out of the ordinary. The stunts these freaks in here can pull leave a grin on his face sometimes. Take the twins who can start a fire just by putting their minds to it. The day they caused the doctor's lunchbox to burst into flames was a high point. All the so-called residents here can be kind of unruly at times; but then who can blame them?

The guard observes the doctor in question being led into her office, and scratches his behind. If he was a kid who found he could make objects move just by touching his temples, or saw things happening behind locked doors, he'd question whether this outfit really had his best interests at heart too. The Foundation may have been set up to help these youngsters get to grips with their abilities, but some of the things Mr Aleister put them through didn't seem to benefit anyone but him. His obsession with the churches was a case in point. How many times had he been asked to chaperone some kid to a crypt or a nave, only to stand back while old baldy had words with them? Whatever was said seemed to scare up half of them, even bring them to tears. He didn't like it, but then he was paid to keep the kids in order, not make a fuss about their welfare.

Reflecting on his time here, the guard attempts to pick his pants from the crack of his backside. This place may be tough on the residents at times, he thinks, but it was a jammy job in one paradise of a building. Keeping watch from this, the upper viewing gallery, was the post they all wanted. It was bathed with sunshine on a good day, and had a glorious view of the stars on a clear night. Best of all you were up here on your own. You could take a nap if you wished, and nobody would be any the wiser.

A soft thumping sound disturbs the guard's thoughts just then. He turns from the balcony, but there's nothing to see. Just parlour palms to break up the curving marble wall, with trunks too thin for anyone to hide behind. He shakes his head, figuring it's probably the girl below working out the last of her tantrum – throwing things at the ceiling with that weird light-force of hers. He glances at his wristwatch, and is pleased to see that it's nearly time for a tea break. After doing nothing for so long, he thinks with a private smile, it would be good to sit down for a while.

On the other side of the balcony, a boy dangles from the lowest rail and prays this guy doesn't look down to his left. Yoshi tightens his grip, tries not to breathe too loudly. Both palms are still stinging from where they had slapped around the rail and stopped him from turning to ketchup on the lobby floor. A *monkey fling*. That was the name of the move he had just executed. It had sprung into his mind in midair, which wasn't a good time to disturb his concentration. First Yoshi had lowered himself through the skylight, then rocked back and forth to build up momentum. On the final swing, he had let go, spread his arms and fixed his sights on the rail. The foliage hanging from the balcony had served to cushion his arrival. He had figured it might also be strong enough to serve as a safety net should he miss. Which he hadn't. Much to his relief.

The question Yoshi asks himself now is just how

long can he hang around? Above him, the guard sounds kind of restless. The boy dares to glance up, and sees the guy shaking one leg as if trying to straighten out his trousers. He closes his eyes, his arms beginning to ache, and then opens them smartly when a squeak of jackboot soles on marble suggests it's time to seize the moment.

This is the true test. Not of skill but of strength. With the guard leaving his post, Yoshi has just seconds to haul himself up and over the balcony. He lands soundlessly, having removed his shoes before making the leap. Forward thinking is what it takes to be a free runner, and Yoshi can't afford to put a foot wrong. His shoes are strung around his shoulders now, and bump about as he flits across the floor to catch up with the guard.

Of all the things he has learned from his time with the crew, this manoeuvre is something he picked up just by watching. He's seen one young punk in action on the streets of Covent Garden, and now it's his turn to try it out – the art of shadowing. The big difference between the set-up for a trick and what he's doing here is that he can't afford to bail out or get it wrong. Yoshi knows he has to be invisible, which means mimicking the man's moves so closely that they practically become one.

One sugar or two? That's all the guard is thinking as he ambles towards the elevator. He's only travelling to the level below, but, well, taking the stairs would eat into his break time. Whistling to himself now, he punches the button on the panel beside the doors. His number takes a while to light up, and so he seizes this opportunity to really pick at the seat of his pants while nobody is looking.

The doors are made from brushed steel. The guard can seen his own reflection, just about. It's a bit blurry, and makes him look like he should be eating a little less dessert. So much so that he sucks in his gut and turns side on just to make sure. The lift arrives with a ping, and the doors slide apart before he's had a chance to resign himself to the fact that this job has turned him into a tubby. Unfortunately, he discovers with a heavy heart, the three interior walls of the lift are fitted with mirrors from floor to ceiling.

22
BACK FOR YOU

Yoshi is so close to the guard that he can smell his body odour. The cheesy reek trails him like the boy himself, silently and invisibly. Every step and scratch the guard makes, Yoshi mirrors the move. Every sudden turn at the doors, the boy swivels around and out of his line of sight. It isn't until they're in the lift that Yoshi becomes aware of the fact that he can see himself on both sides.

One false move, he thinks to himself, *this show is over*.

The guard abandons the tune he's been whistling so badly, and turns to punch the button for his floor. With no desire to look at himself too closely – given the extra pounds he's packing – he's happy to focus on the balcony he's about to leave behind. Just as the doors begin to shut, however, he swears something doesn't look quite right with the skylight. He scratches at his behind one final time, cursing the condition he's suffering back there on account of all that sitting between shifts, and decides he'll investigate this level later. Later. After a nice cup of tea and a biscuit.

Yoshi's senses feel like lasers, the way he's forced to focus on every sudden move. He feels scared being this close to someone who could do him harm, and also very stupid. If this blimp were a statue, it wouldn't be so hard to hide behind him. But he isn't made of stone. He's flesh, blood and bone, like him. Flesh, blood and bone that could simply squash him flat if he knew what is going on behind his back.

The boy breathes out at the same time as the doors slide open. He's made it to the floor he wants. He knows he is within reach of the room where the girl must have faced up to that woman in the white coat. It's getting there that could be a problem, as the guard moves out before the boy is ready, and turns in the opposite direction. For one long moment, Yoshi is left feeling exposed and startled. Several guards occupy this floor, some of whom nod at the man he has shadowed this far. The boy's heart begins to pound. He flexes his fingers, feeling thrilled but also chilled to be operating without cover, and then reaches for the shoes strung around his neck. There's only one way out, the boy decides. With the shoes in one hand now, he twirls them like a pair of karate nunchucks, and then flings them as far as he can.

Yoshi watches the lace-bound shoes helicopter over the head of the guard looking out over the atrium. The crash that follows occurs one, maybe two levels down. It sounds like a display vase breaking, certainly something precious, and is enough to draw the attention of every goon the boy can see.

"What the heck was that?"

"Go check it out, Butch."

"What if it's one of the whacko kids? I don't trust 'em, boss. They all must have heard the argument just now. You know what those kids can be like when it comes to settling scores. I'm not going to walk into a set-up and come back jibbering and drooling like a baby. I've seen what mind-tricks they can pull when they're angry. We should go together."

"Butch, come here a moment."

"What is it, boss— ouch!"

"You think a poke in the eye hurts? That's nothin'! I'm ashamed to be your superior! Now fall in behind me, and if any of those suckers look at me funny, you get me out of there sharpish. Is that clear?"

"Yessir!"

Watching this security spat from the elevator, and with a light shining on him from above, Yoshi prays these bickering guards aren't as lazy as the sloth he just used to get this far. With baited breath, he watches them leave their posts now. To his great relief, they head for the stairs. Not only that, they skirt the balcony with their attention fixed on the point where his shoes have landed. *Misdirection.* That was the secret of making magic, according to Mikhail, and it might just have worked here.

With the guards out of the frame, Yoshi breaks from the elevator, and finds himself facing a whole sweep of rooms around the atrium. What's more, all of them have doors half open and the same house lights shining from the inside. Just then, voices rise up from a floor below. The guards must be sensing that all is not as it seems, he fears, judging by their air of urgency. Instinctively, and knowing he has no time to lose, Yoshi heads for the room with an unusually bright light. The boy hesitates outside, concerned by what he might find. He even straightens out his shirt, as if conscious of the impression he's about to make. With a deep breath, he steps over the threshold. With what sounds like a gasp from inside, the light floods and brightens.

"Yoshi?" It's a girl's voice, sounding familiar but cautious.

"Apparently I told you I'd be back," he says with a grin, upon which this unusual glow begins to warm and then flicker, as if he's found himself facing a welcoming hearth fire.

190

23

LET THERE BE LIGHT

The last time Livia saw Yoshi, Aleister had been snapping at his heels. The boy's escape may not have been planned, but she was unsurprised when it happened. "Where have you *been*?" she asks him now, and dries her cheeks with the heel of her hand.

Yoshi pretends not to notice, despite having found her weeping at the edge of her bed. "Around town," he says, tensing when she hugs him and plants a kiss on his cheek. "In places you wouldn't believe."

She senses his discomfort and pulls away to meet his eyes. "What's happened? You can tell me. We always tell each other everything. You look like you don't even know who I am, Yoshi. It's me. Livia."

"I don't really know myself," he confesses. "My memory took a few knocks."

The haze around her head and shoulders turns a melancholy blue.

"He got to you, didn't he?"

"The bald guy? He came close," Yoshi says to reassure her. "Luckily some friends got to me first."

Aleister had been pushing him for ages. Every day, he would show up at the Foundation, shrug his stupid showy coat from his shoulders, and fast-track the boy through the programme to perfect the control of his powers. He did the same thing with all the kids who showed real promise, but this unlucky lad seemed to earn the greatest attention. Like almost everyone here, the gift he had was both a blessing and a curse. Some said such psychic abilities were a freak of nature. Others believed it was nature's way of making the human race aware of other universal energies. All the kids expressed their powers in different ways, but all of them found it shaped their lives – for better and for worse.

Livia herself had lived in a sphere of translucent light for several years now. Everyone talked of the changes you went through in your teens, but none of her friends had experienced *this*. For months, Livia had been referred from one doctor to the next, but nobody could diagnose what was causing it. One thing she knew for certain, it singled her out in the very worst way. Her friends became wary, and boys would not go near her. Especially when it became clear that the light changed in colour, contrast and hue according to her emotional state.

Any other girl could keep a lid on a crush. Not Livia. Any hint of feeling shone through in the form of this remarkable haze, and she had quickly withdrawn from the world around. So, when her father found details of this place from a colleague in the city, she had been only too willing to enrol.

"How did you get back inside the building?" she whispers to Yoshi now, closing the door with a click. "The guards see everything!"

He smiles, unsure where to begin. "A kind of magic," is all he can say.

"You'll never leave alive if Aleister catches you here."

"It's a flying visit," Yoshi tells her. "Come on. We should get going. There's so much to see beyond these walls!"

Livia's father had been sold on the idea of a residential stay. According to the prospectus, the Foundation's aim was to help young people like her come to terms with what was happening to them. It was, according to the written testimonials at the back, an opportunity for "unconventionally gifted" children to discover themselves in order to live a full and rewarding life. As Livia had spent many years at boarding school, including the last intolerable term, when her aura seriously blossomed, it seemed worth a shot at least. Even so, for all the anonymous profiles of graduates who had tamed their psychic talents, something about this outfit didn't feel right. By then, however, Livia's father had paid the fees. He would miss his daughter with all his heart, but it was a price worth paying to rid her of what he once called "the unfortunate side of her inheritance".

As soon as Livia had said her tearful goodbye at the Foundation's electric gates, knowing she would have no further contact with her family until the people in white coats signed her back into their care, her suspicions began to burn bright. Aleister was at the heart of her misgivings. As the Director, he was as charming as his presence was imposing. He had explained that as a teenager he too had lived in the shadow of his psychic gift: an awareness of the natural forces vibrating through every atom of life. As a young man, so he told her, he had seen such energies everywhere, and over time it drove him insane. Locked in a world of his own, he had relied on church soup kitchens, and kept a pet snake in his pocket so sneak thieves couldn't fleece him of what pennies he could beg. Had it not been for a determination to get well and help others as he had helped himself, this Foundation would never exist. Livia had listened to every word of his story, and her aura had softened with each sentence. She had felt pity for his plight, and then admiration, but still something left her wary. This man had certainly been to a dark place in his life, but his manner with the kids here made her question whether he might still be revisiting it.

Then came the tests and exercises. Starting the next day. As soon as she was led into the room with the equipment, and saw the headgear lying on the seat of the chair, Livia had panicked and asked to go home. Aleister had assured her it was merely a monitor, designed to detect electrical changes in the brain, but in Livia's eyes it was all too much too soon. It made her realise that her aura was a problem for other people, not her. It was a part of who she was, and she would much prefer to live with it than go through this. That's when she'd seen another side to Aleister. When his patience snapped without warning, she had submitted to his will in fear for her life. The test seemed to sap her spark and energy. It left her with a headache, and a livid aura that did not subside for days. From that moment on, Livia had thought of little else but getting out of here. With guards stationed in the building and the grounds, however, the prospect of escape seemed hopeless. Even now, facing the boy who had managed to get away and then break back in, she can't fathom how he did it.

"OK, hotshot," she says. "Show me the way out of this hellhole."

Yoshi scans the room, finds a window like the one he went through the first time. "Well—"

"Don't even think about it!" Livia informs him. "*You* might be comfortable flinging yourself across the rooftops – Parkour was pretty much your whole life before they locked you up here, after all – only this is no time for that lesson you promised."

"But I made it here on instinct," he tells her. "You can do it too – you really just need to believe in yourself."

As her stay at the foundation turned from days to weeks, Livia had made friends with the other residents. It helped in many ways, reminding her that she was not alone in feeling both confused and violated by the agenda here. The trips to the churches were what really mystified them all. Aleister admitted that it bought back troubling memories of the time when he'd been forced to rely on the grace of their soup kitchens. Indeed, he even confessed that he'd eventually found his own salvation from the streets and the madness that consumed him. And yet despite it all, he'd regularly drag them off on excursions to one of seven sacred locations around London.

Livia herself found she quite enjoyed the trips. At the very least, it meant being free from the Foundation for a while. Aleister and the guards always kept a close eye on her, but it was peaceful in those churches, and it gave her time to think. Others seriously objected. None more so than the boy who had come to be her closest friend in the nine months she had been a resident. He might have taken off recently, surprising everyone but Livia, but he stood before her now.

He had arrived just weeks after her, and been assigned living quarters on the other side of the atrium. Even so, once they got to know each other in the canteen, he would visit her regularly in her room just by closing his eyes and concentrating. Remote viewing was what the specialists called his psychic gift. At first, Livia had been deeply mistrustful of any boy who could peek through closed doors and curtains, but then she had got to know him, and come to trust his sense of decency. It also helped that Livia could feel his presence when his mind's eye opened on her quarters. This way they would spend hours shooting the breeze, sharing jokes and spinning stories, and just keeping each other company, despite being in different rooms. Livia had confided that she came from aristocracy. It was a fact she tended to hide from most people, uncomfortable as she was with her landed wealth and privilege. In return, the boy who was the first to stand up to Aleister and flee from his control, promised her one thing. When they were both free, he would teach the girl a way of life that would allow her to scale to great heights with her determination, passion, grace and skill.

"If I jump, I die," she informs the young parkour now. "I trust my instincts just as you trust yours, and right now mine are screaming at me to keep my feet on the ground."

"Livia, it's our only hope!"

"Believe me," she says, "I desperately want out as much as you do. It's just I'd like to live to tell the tale."

Yoshi stares at her, thinking hard. "Do you know how to make yourself invisible?" he asks finally.

"Excuse me?" Livia frowns, one corner of her mouth all bunched up now like she's unsure whether or not to burst out laughing. "OK, so how do I disappear?" she asks, like this is some kind of joke. "If there's a risk that bones could be broken then you can forget it."

The evening Yoshi had taken off, following a furious row with Aleister, Livia had wondered if she'd ever see him again. Yoshi had made his escape through an open window. Just vaulted over the sill like a spur-of-the-moment suicide, and disappeared from view. Livia remembered seeing the Director and his team crowd the window in a panic. With so much greenery in the beds and rockeries below, however, none of them could see whether the boy had survived such a fall. Then one of the counsellors had chanced to glance up, and spotted the young wall-hopper shinning up a drainpipe.

Only Aleister had climbed out in pursuit, roaring at the kid to get down and face the music. The Director had come close as well, but then even he must have resigned himself to the fact that this was Yoshi's territory. Livia had lingered at the window, and returned there at every opportunity. When she had sensed him viewing her remotely, she knew it wouldn't be long before he showed up for real. Now here he is, asking if she knows how to make herself vanish! It seems it isn't just his memory Yoshi has lost. His marbles have gone missing, too.

"Livia, I'm not suggesting we can get out of here in a puff of smoke. I'm talking about falling in so closely behind your target that they can't see you. It's called shadowing."

"Look at me," she says, stopping Yoshi there and drawing his attention to her aura. It's cooled a little since his arrival, but still flickers and pulses around her. "Do I look like the kind of person who can blend in with a crowd?"

Yoshi registers her point with some embarrassment. "OK, in that case there's only one way out of here."

"And what way is that?"

"Through the main entrance."

"First you want me to shimmy behind the guards. Now you think we should simply stroll down to the lobby and wave goodbye as we leave? That's even crazier than your shadowing idea." She taps her temple. "Is everything working upstairs, Yoshi?"

The boy smiles and turns for the door. "Not quite," he replies, "but I'm feeling more like myself by the minute."

24

WATCH CLOSELY

Yoshi has no clear plan this time. Nor does he have any more tricks up his sleeve. All he takes with him is an instinct to survive and a girl who wears her emotions on the outside. Creeping back into the corridor, the glow surrounding her turns amber like a warning beacon. She grips his hand. He leads her several steps across the floor, upon which that light around her suddenly switches to red.

"We can't just leave!" she hisses.

"What do you mean?" Yoshi looks around nervously. At any moment the guards are going to be back on this level like bloodhounds. Throwing his shoes over the balcony has distracted them all right. Once found, however, those goons will know they have been fooled. He faces the girl again, takes her by both hands this time. "Livia, if we hang around we're history. This is our only chance!"

"I'm thinking of the others!" She begins to pull him back. This time, it's the compassion in her eyes, not the colour of her aura, that spells out her reluctance to leave. "Don't they deserve a chance, too?"

Slowly, Yoshi's attention turns to the vast horseshoe of half-open doors flanking the one they've just left. It takes a moment for him to register the curious but frightened-looking faces now peering from each of these rooms. None of the others leave their quarters, as if too scared to cross that threshold. Instead they simply stand and stare at the pair.

"I know you," breathes Yoshi, as if consulting his memory. "You all look so familiar."

Livia frees herself from his hands. "You really have gone gaga, haven't you?"

"OK," he whispers finally, aware that time is pressing. "If we all go together perhaps we can charge our way out. Follow me!"

He turns for the balcony, hoping to scope out the guards' position before breaking for the stairs, only to come right round again when one of the kids hisses, "*No!*"

"What now?" says Yoshi, in both frustration and fear.

"There's no time for second thoughts," adds Livia, equally bemused. "Isn't this what we've all been waiting for?"

"*Please!*" Yoshi says, practically begging now. "If we don't get to those stairs in the next few seconds, the guards will be back on this floor and we'll lose our advantage. At least if we all go as one we can bundle our way to the lobby."

The kid in question shakes his head. "I'm not coming!" he squeaks. "I don't want Aleister to get mad with me." He's young, this lad, with bottle-bottom glasses that magnify his frightened eyes. Yoshi also notes the faint trace of an aura around him. The kid's psychic powers might be in an early stage of development, but his terror has clearly overwhelmed him.

"You *have* to come!" pleads Livia. "It's the moment we've all been waiting for."

There's another little one beside this kid with the glasses. He drops away a step and looks at his shoes. "Count me out as well."

"Me too," concedes another voice, further along the row, which quickly turns into a chorus. Yoshi watches, aghast, as one child after another retreats into their room, until just one door is left open.

One door with two girls, standing side by side.

Two girls who appear to be identical in appearance, from their hipster jeans, chain-link belts and high-cut tops. They look about fifteen, at a guess, though it's safe to say there's only seconds between them. Even the way they appear to size up the boy seems cut from the same cloth. If it weren't for one striking difference, there'd be no telling them apart.

"I'm with you," says the girl whose long hair has

been braided with red and silver beads. She speaks with a tough American accent, but what impresses Yoshi more than anything is the fact that she's volunteered. "Aleister might scare me, but I like to think that sometimes I can scare him back a little bit!"

"Where she goes," echoes the one with the blue beads instead of red, "I go, too."

Yoshi glances questioningly at Livia, who flattens her lips and says, "If your memory is really that muddled, you need me more than you think. Yoshi, meet Scarlett and Blaize."

"You're twins, right?" says Yoshi, wishing he could remember more about them. "From the States?"

"Well spotted, genius." Livia smiles wryly, then turns to address the two girls. "Before Yoshi makes an even bigger fool of himself, perhaps you'd like to remind him what qualifies you to be here for so-called treatment."

"We don't have much time," says Yoshi fretfully.

"It'll be over in a flash," says the red-beaded twin called Scarlett, turning to high-five her sister. As their palms connect, bright flames snap out from in between and then vaporise immediately. "It's called pyrokenesis."

"We're firestarters," says Blaize to explain, sounding almost triumphant. "Sometimes I get mad with people, and before they know it they're wondering why the soles of their shoes have started smouldering."

"Back home in the Bronx," says Scarlett, taking over now, "when the juvenile court ordered us here for treatment, the press dubbed us the Sizzle Sisters."

"Don't ever call us that, though," her sister warns. "We don't warm to nicknames."

"*Shh!*" This is Yoshi, cringing at the noise they're making. "Girls, that's hot stuff you just did there, but let's save the rest for later. If you're with us, let's go!" He turns, dropping low to cross to the balcony, and is relieved this time that all three fall in behind.

What's not so heartening is the sound of boots heading up the steps towards them. Yoshi keeps on moving, aware that whoever it is has only just begun climbing. He reaches the balcony and signals for everyone to stay low.

"What now?" breathes Livia, clearly rattled.

Suddenly, Yoshi finds all eyes on him. He glances between the balcony rails, through the hanging foliage. What he sees are several guards down there examining the shoes he'd thrown, and one making his way up to this floor.

"Someone give me a shoe," he says, appealing to them all.

"What happened to yours?" asks Blaize.

205

Yoshi glances at his toes, sensing an explanation will just take too long. "I jump better in bare feet," is all he says.

"Will you stop talking about jumping?" Livia looks at him fiercely. "What you do is a death wish, Yoshi. Like I told you the first time, I don't have a problem with pavements. You can take a *running* jump if you like. I'd sooner stay here and watch."

"I need a shoe *now!*" he hisses so urgently that all three volunteer. Scarlett is the first to oblige, kicking off both pumps. With no time to explain himself, Yoshi grabs one, lobs it like a hand grenade, and ducks out of sight.

Even before the shoe has dropped into the atrium, a shout goes up from below.

"There! One of the freaks! Get him!"

"Run!" yells Yoshi, breaking cover now, and again imploring the girls to follow. Immediately, the building transforms into a hive of panic. There are guards shouting, footfalls echoing everywhere and kids at their doors once more, screaming at the three would-be escapees to run for their lives. And yet, despite it all, Yoshi hears only Mikhail's advice about magic and illusion replaying in his mind. His stunt with the shoe might have misdirected the guards once. This time, it has served to alert every single one of them to their presence.

Never pull the same trick twice. That's what the young Russian had warned him, and this kind of uproar from an audience was the reason why.

"There's no way out!" Livia tells him. Her aura is pulsing now, like a heart working overtime. "We're finished!"

Yoshi implores them all to keep up, only to backtrack when the first guard appears at the top of the stairs. He falters on the last step, and then focuses on all three escapees. But before he's summoned the wit to call out to his colleagues, the light around Livia begins to regroup. It seems to flow in front of her face, as if taking instruction from behind her closed eyes now.

"Don't hurt him!" pleads Scarlett, as this strange illumination stretches towards the guard. Meantime Blaize detects another one approaching from their blind side. She spins around and scowls.

"Stay back, buddy, or you're toast!" This guard advances by a step, only to lift his foot from the floor like he's suddenly walked onto a bed of coals. Several others pull up behind him. Blaize's sister, Scarlett, issues the same threat at them, although she doesn't seem so sure of herself. Even Livia is faltering. Her aura has brightened so intensely that her target has to look away, but there are yet more guards spilling up the stairs.

"We're outnumbered!" Yoshi yells, trying to keep

an eye on them all. Slowly, the security force begins to circle and close around them. The boy glances at Livia. She meets his eyes through her haze, which is thinning by the second.

"I'm sorry," she says. "I'm sorry I called you back here."

"Don't say that!" he tells her, and turns to glare at these uniformed thugs. "I discovered who I am thanks to you," he adds. "There's no way I'm leaving your side now."

"Give it up, guys," says one of the guards. It's the oversized one who Yoshi had shadowed earlier, and he's sweating badly. "Aleister is on his way here right now. If he finds everyone is home as they should be, maybe he'll go easy on us all." He stops there to address one of his colleagues. "Get the rooms on lockdown," he mutters, glancing at the horseshoe of conspicuously closed doors. "I can't afford to lose any more freaks."

Yoshi glares at him, then shoots one desperate glance at the skylight high overhead. There's no human way that anyone could get up to it, let alone three kids who have never taken to the rooftops as he has. Just then, the deadening sound of bolts crashing informs the boy that all the rooms behind them have now become out of bounds. He considers scrambling for the balcony, if only to give the girls a chance to slip away. But even if he had the courage to leap for it, gravity would drag him down – and with a deadly splash to finish. That water feature in the lobby certainly hadn't looked deeper than a bath, thinks Yoshi, though it isn't what happened to the woman in the white coat that persuades him to stay put. It's the draining sound – a great gurgling that rises through the atrium now, as if a giant plug has come unstuck.

The guards are first to react, glancing around in turn. Yoshi sees some break away, drawn by the interruption. They lean cautiously over the balcony, and then turn to one another in shock and disbelief.

"What's happening?" asks Livia. "Something's going on below us."

"There's a *lot* going on below us," says Yoshi, wishing they could just magic themselves back to the bunker. Only then does he consider what's just popped out of his mouth. "In fact," he adds, sounding brighter all of a sudden, "Something big may just be about to surface."

Even as he speaks, yet more guards turn to investigate the commotion. Only the big guy is left squaring up to them, but it's clear the disturbance is troubling him. Finally, he abandons this face-off to take a look, which prompts the boy and his friends to do likewise.

And way down there, breaking the surface of

the tropical water feature in the lobby, what looks to one and all like a swamp monster delivers an anguished howl.

25

SHADOW SIEGE

"Boss, I don't like what I'm looking at here. Whatever's underneath all that weed and slime is mad as hell!"

"Stay cool, people."

"Could it be one of the freaks, messing with our minds?"

"Why don't you go and find out, Butch."

"Me? Why me? It's always me!"

"Because then I don't have to listen to you whinnying like a lost pony!"

"But Boss—"

"Do as I say!"

As the guards continue to bicker, betraying their fear and confusion, Yoshi turns to his friends and whispers, "It's OK."

"How can you say that?" asks Scarlett, her eyes locked on the wailing beast.

The pond is little more than a puddle now, exposing this tortured creature from the deep. Its face is streaked by muddy silt, like some kind of tribal war paint. As it fights to be free from the weed through which it has risen, all that can be seen are two angry eyes.

"I just can't believe what I'm seeing," her sister offers.

Yoshi thinks back to the lessons he learned in the bunker, and begins to understand what's going on. "It's a weapon of mass delusion," he tells them, and just prays that he is right. "By playing to the crowd, it's less likely that anyone will dare to question what's going on. We should use the opportunity to get away before someone braves speaking up."

"We really should make that move *now*," breathes Livia, her attention still locked on the abomination below. "Everyone is watching it, so if we're going to leave let's make it right away."

Yoshi is set to creep under the guards' noses, only for this beast from the deep to stop thrashing and face the audience on several galleries. A hush falls over the atrium, but instead of roaring some more, it clears its throat and, in a voice suited for the stage, asks: "Is Yoshi in the building?"

The guard closest to the boy, the twitchy one called Butch, comes alive in response and shouts, "Here he is!" Yoshi peers over the balcony. This time, he sees a familiar face behind the muck. "Go to him," Butch whispers, clearly sold on what's happening here. Yoshi glances at the other guards. If any of them have doubts about what's going on, their gullible colleague has just made it harder for them to speak up. "He's come for you," Butch whispers to the boy. "*Sacrifice* yourself!"

"If I go," says Yoshi, playing to the crowd himself now, and jabs a thumb over this shoulder, "my three friends here come with me."

"Don't lay down demands!" Butch hisses. "Just do as it asks!"

"Nobody is going anywhere!" This is the guard Butch had called boss. His uniform is no different to the others, but his baseball cap sports seven stars of rank across the bill. The look on his face tells Yoshi this charade might be over sooner than he had hoped. "Aleister will be here any minute now!" he bellows. "If he finds that order has broken down, we'll all be fired. Butch, I don't intend to tell you again. Get down to the lobby and eject this idiot from the premises. It's no monster. Be a man and admit you were fooled for a moment. Just look at what's freaking you out here. It's some skinny toerag badly in need of a clean up."

The monster in question acts hurt all of a sudden. He points at himself, looks over his shoulder just to check the guard hadn't intended to insult anyone else. "You didn't want to say that," he declares, shaking one foot after the other to lose the clinging weed. "You really ought to apologise, or face the consequences."

The girls glance at Yoshi, seemingly unimpressed, but he knows just what's going on. This beast may have revealed his true nature, but in doing so he's continuing to draw the guards in. Cautiously, Yoshi begins to size up their escape routes. "We'll go on my word," he whispers to Livia and the twins, still watching the dripping-wet figure below and wondering how far he might take it.

"Don't push me," the beast warns the boss guard. "I've seen a lot of sewage on my way here, followed by an unexpected downpour when I spun the hatch just now. Nobody told me I'd find two tonnes of murky water on top of it. My brief was to make a surprise entrance. I didn't expect the surprise to be on *me*! So, sir, if you'd care to show some politeness at least, we can leave here without anyone getting hurt."

The guard chuckles for a moment. He clears his throat to regain control, but it's no good. He guffaws loudly, his eyes shining in a bid to keep it together, and then laughs so hard that those guards around him swap goofy, nervous glances.

"What's so funny?" asks Livia, as the laughter quickly spreads. "There's no excuse for bad manners."

"Never mind that." Yoshi gestures for the girls to follow him. "Let's go!"

The boy moves lightly on his feet, using the commotion as cover. Nearing the stairs, he glances back to check the others are close behind. When he faces forward once more, he only has time to gasp before crashing into something solid that's just blocked his path. It's the boss guard. A man who is laughing harder than anyone else, but who must have been watching their every move. And now here he is, still chortling away, but with one strong hand clamped around the boy's arm.

"You should stick around," he tells Yoshi, still cracking up at what seems to him like one lame attempt at a rescue bid. "You'll miss the best bit, when this clown gets ejected from the premises. It'll give you a taster of the kind of kicking we have in mind for you."

Below, the so-called swamp monster is mashing through the puddles left in the water feature. "You leave them alone!" he warns, jabbing a finger accusingly. "My friends will be joining us at any moment. And they really don't like it when people pick on me, or anyone else!"

The boss guard rocks back on his heels at this. He's seriously tickled, even if his crack team of security professionals appear more baffled than anything else. They're laughing along with him, but

215

really do so just to fit in. For they're also swapping nervous glances with one another, plainly unsure what's going on. All in all it's a grand distraction. Whatever they make of this uprising through the slime and the weeds, sheer bravado is what has disarmed these guards so effectively. Yoshi wriggles in vain to free himself from the security chief – the only guard to lose himself to laughter and yet maintain his authority – while the girls look on in despair.

"Easy now!" this boss guard warns Yoshi, recovering his composure for a moment. "You'll really have to try harder next time."

The boy looks up into his sniggering face, and hangs his head in defeat. *That's it*, he thinks to himself. *This show is over*. He mouths an apology at the swamp monster down there, who shrugs like he gave it his best shot. Then, much to the surprise of Yoshi and the girls, the monster takes a step back to assist a second figure from the drain hole – a raggedy old lion of a man, looking half-lost but strangely pleased to be here. More so, in fact, as the laughter and uproar sounding from every level falls away to silence.

"*Julius!*" cries Yoshi, twisting helplessly under the boss guard's grip.

"What's with the pensioner?" asks Blaize, with a note of derision. "Is he here to hand out toffees?"

On the bed of the former swamp, overlooked by several floors and illuminated by the ambient lighting like a scooped stage in the round, Julius Grimaldi steps up to address his rapt audience.

"Please forgive my young friend here for kicking up such a stink," he says, but thinks twice about clapping the swamp monster on the shoulder. "When I asked brave Billy here to spin open the hatch I believed only wires and cables would spill out. Had I known it wasn't a service hatch, I would've asked him to find another point to surface."

Billy No-Beard rids himself of yet more slime with a pointed flick of his wrists. "It's the last time I go first," he mutters, and faces up to Yoshi once again. "In fact," he suggests, with the hint of a glint in his eye, "why don't *you* show us the way out of here?"

"Nobody goes anywhere!" This is the boss guard, who demonstrates he means business by crooking his arm around Yoshi's throat. "Butch, for the last time, I'm ordering you to the lobby. Escort these jokers from the premises, and have the water feature refilled immediately. If Aleister's precious ecosystem has been disturbed, it could end up brimming with our blood."

"Understood, boss!"

Butch heads for the steps that would take him to

the water feature, eager to follow orders. He barely moves, however, before Julius cries, "You really don't want to come any closer, young man. Not if you know what's waiting in the wings at this moment!"

Yoshi hears this and gives up struggling against the boss guard. If there's a chance that Julius can outwit the guards then this is it. He checks that Livia and the twins are watching, sees their eyes widen at what creeps from every hallway in the lobby.

"I'm scared," says Livia. "Really."

"Me too," breathes Scarlett. "What are we looking at here?"

"Well?" asks Blaize, glaring at the boy. "This had better be good!"

The mood lamps in the lobby are designed to foreground the water feature and the mangrove around it. They shine in from the surrounding hallways, cutting the walls with slanting light. Looking down from the balcony, it's impossible to see where each hallway leads. All that can be seen is the beam shining from each one, strong enough to throw down a shadow to forewarn of another presence. Yoshi is just wondering where the rest of the crew might be stationed, when something happens that makes sense of things for him. For as Julius Grimaldi and the Executive Deck Hand turn slowly in opposite directions, so a pack of looming shadows stalk into the light.

"Now," says Billy, wiping his cheeks clean with his fingertips, "are you going to let Yoshi and his friends come forward, or do we have to unleash the dogs?"

A growl strikes up from one of the hallways next, quickly matched by others.

"They sound big," a guard near Yoshi observes, and then whimpers when the shadows begin to shape into the pointed ears and pinched eyes of a wild-looking dog indeed. "Very big!"

"Stay calm!" comes the order from the boss guard. "It's just another illusion," he assures them, but it's clear that even he doesn't sound so certain this time. By now, the lights have revealed an entire pack. They might be hanging back in the darkness, but the shadows on the walls suggest these dogs look set to leap. "I'm a trained handler," the boss calls out next, clearly hoping that might make them go away. "I didn't make it to the top in the security business without knowing how to handle big dogs."

As if in response, one of the shadows appears to rise up on hind legs and walk like a human.

"Those are no dogs!" splutters Butch, backing away from the rail as yet more dark, canine shapes reform against the wall.

"You're right," says Yoshi, keen to get in on the act if it means one last chance at escape. "They're *werewolves!*"

His claim draws looks of disbelief from the girls, but it's all too much for Butch and several other guards. They take off in a hurry, deaf to the threats from their superior.

"Werewolves are a myth!" rages the boss guard, furious that so many of his men are deserting their posts. With his nostrils flaring under the bill of his cap, he throws Yoshi to one side and storms for the stairs. "But you two jokers will be *history* when I get my hands on you!"

"OK, I admit it!" Billy shows him his palms, stalling him at the top of the stairs. "These are not werewolves."

Julius seems surprised by this admission. Even some of the shadows fall back on all fours, ears pricked and heads cocked in confusion.

"So, what *have* you got hidden down there?" asks the boss guard, his curiosity beginning to overtake his anger.

"You don't want know," warns Billy, though he seems unsure what to add.

Julius frowns. Billy shrugs. The pair look like actors who have lost their lines.

Slowly, the boss guard begins his descent of the stairs. "I do believe you're bluffing," he growls, and signals at those who value their jobs to step in line now.

"Let them go!" Yoshi calls out, ignoring this clear chance to get away, but the boss is deaf to them now. Down below, the old man in the patchwork coat and the mud-caked kid beside him look as if they have been struck by stage fright. "I'll do whatever you say, but don't hurt them," pleads the boy, concerned only for the safety of Julius and Billy. They might belong to a crew he's only just fallen in with, but they've also come to mean a great deal to him, he realises with his next breath. "I'm begging you to let them go," he yells. "They're like . . . like *family* to me!"

26

A SHOW OF STRENGTH

The boss guard halts at the foot of the stairs. He rests a hand on each banister, as if to restrain all those behind him.

"Give it up," he barks at Billy. "Stop making a spectacle of yourself."

"Spectacle?" Billy shoots a finger to the air. "I'll give you a *spectacle*!" The look on his face tells Yoshi that he's only just conjured up what he's about to say. Even so, he seems very confident all of a sudden. Stepping forward now, Billy cups one hand to his mouth as if to conspire with his audience. "What we have here," he reveals, pointing at the gloomy hallways, "is a rare sight, both feared and revered by the residents of Chinatown." The shadows on the walls shift and flex, as if the creatures lurking back there are growing restless. "You may think the kids here are freaks," continues Billy, in his element now, "but you won't know the meaning of the word until you've seen what I am about to summon up."

"No!" shouts Julius, stepping forward himself. "If you give the word these fiends will slay every single one of us!"

"Then give us what we want!" Billy demands, addressing the balconies still. "Otherwise, we'll take our chances!"

"Billy!" the old man hisses, looking very scared all of a sudden. "This is a lobby, not a gladiatorial arena!"

The boss guard remains at the foot of the stairs, breathing heavily through flared nostrils.

"No deal!" he says, glaring at Billy from under his peaked cap. "Bring it on, my friend. It's high time this pantomime came to an end."

"Pantomime?" For a second time, Billy clutches his heart as if a knife has just been thrust in. "This is no pantomime, sir. We're here for our friends, by any means possible. Consider this a show of *strength*!"

"Don't do it," hisses Julius, standing behind him like some dignitary's interpreter, but it's too late now.

"You leave me no choice!" Billy is beginning to get a little carried away, thinks Yoshi, but even he takes a sharp intake of breath, along with everyone else, when the Executive Deck Hand steps up onto the biggest boulder in this former water feature. There, he crouches on one knee and then flings out his hands as if casting some kind of spell: "Feast your eyes on the infamous . . . Opium Vampires!"

All heads turn just as Billy has directed. The first thing that happens is the silhouettes disappear. Just snap back into the gloom and vanish. Then, from somewhere in the deeper reaches of the hall, a scraping sound can be heard, like a dead foot dragging behind a good one. At the same time, a twist of purple smoke creeps into the atrium. This is followed by a shadow that crosses both the wall and the floor. It's huge, far bigger than before – a muscular torso with what looks like great pointed wings unfolding. The old man is the first to react, shrinking behind Billy and gripping his shoulders fearfully.

"What have you done?" he says, trembling. "Why did you have to bring them *here*?"

The boss guard snorts, but he's clearly not comfortable. He turns to share a comment with the guard behind and finds all of them have melted away. "Hey!" he says, spinning around now. "Don't leave me to handle this alone!"

Billy consults the time. He wipes a smear of mud from his watch face, and says, "If you want to get away with your life, I advise you to head for the exits. These fiends are here for a blood fix. They promised to spare me if I led them to fresh feeding grounds. When I learned about this fine building, all tucked up behind gated gardens, I knew they'd find it hard to resist. You shouldn't have been so secretive about what goes on here, fellas. If something terrible happened, the outside world wouldn't know about it for ages!"

A screech from one of the halls rings around the atrium now. It's a terrible sound, like a high-karate chop from hell, followed by a manic cackle. Yet more talons of purple smoke emerge from other halls now, followed in turn by the shadows of wings as big as yacht sails.

Watching from the balcony, with guards turning tail by the second, Yoshi becomes aware of a slender hand slipping into his own.

"Don't worry," he whispers to Livia, and squeezes tightly. "They're here for us."

She looks at him in horror, as do the twins.

"*Vampires* are here for *us*?"

"That depends," he says under his breath, "on whether you believe in magic."

By now, just a handful of guards remain at the balconies. Most are too dumbstruck to realise their colleagues have deserted them. Down below, the first set of wings opens wide, casting the boss guard in shadow. He looks up with a start at the silhouette before him. Whatever it is seems to float out of the smoke, defying both gravity and reason. He staggers back with a cry, only to snag his heel on the lowest step and sprawl onto his back. Before he knows what's looming over him, Yoshi has grabbed his three friends and is racing for the stairs ... for *this* is their opportunity, with the distraction at its height. Indeed, he doesn't stop for the boss guard at the bottom, and nor do Livia and the twins. One after the other, they trample over the poor man as he tries to stand, the final foot catching him a glancing blow.

"You did it!" Yoshi rushes for this dark and looming apparition, leaving Livia and the twins to stare aghast into the light. "I'm so glad to see you!"

"What can it be?" Blaize asks her sister, who simply watches as the silhouette touches the ground once more, and even seems to shrink by a couple of metres as it steps forward to greet the boy.

"Mikhail!" beams Yoshi. "You make a great vampire!" In each hand, the spike-haired Russian is clutching the corner of a long curtain. When he lets them go, they fall back in place over the long facing windows in the hallway. "Tell me," Yoshi presses him, standing back to get a better look, "how *do* you float on air?"

"Not now, my friend." Mikhail turns his attention to the girls. "I'll teach you how to levitate if you choose to stick with us, but for now let's leave a little to the imagination, huh?"

"Oh go on, *please!*"

"Yoshi, I'm busting to ask how your pretty friend here can make her head light up, but now is not the time to swap illusions."

"Mine isn't an illusion," Livia protests, but Mikhail just smiles like they all say that.

Just as her aura begins to blaze an indignant puce, one of the crew calls out across the lobby. "It's time to pull the troops," he declares, drawing their attention. "Look lively, people!" With his finger pressed to his ear, it's clear he's in touch with the Bridge. At least a dozen rag-tag punks cross the floor now, emerging from the halls where this elaborate shadow play has just been performed. They move with some purpose, like stagehands after a performance.

Yoshi turns to Mikhail. "How did you all get in here? I only saw Billy and Julius climb out of the drain."

The Russian boy smiles, snaps his finger and thumb away to his left. When Yoshi looks back at him, he's holding a bunch of flowers in his other hand.

"Consider it a misdirection master class," says Mikhail, and wheels around to face the twins. "Here's a variation," he adds, and swishes the bunch like a scimitar. It's all too fast for Yoshi, but the resulting split is no surprise to him now.

"Nice move," he says, as Mikhail presents a

bunch to Blaize and then to Scarlett. "Maybe a little bit cheesy, though."

As if to show their agreement, the twins admire their flowers. Their expressions don't change, even when both bunches suddenly wilt, blacken and begin to smoke.

"Oops," says Blaize, and grins at her sister.

"It's the thought that counts," says Scarlett, and drops the burning bunch on the floor.

"Now *that* is what I call a trick!" Mikhail's voice is pitched a mile high. "You girls are cutting edge. Come on, put me in the picture."

"Like you just said," smiles Yoshi. "Now is not the time."

The kid with his ear tuned to the Bridge cuts into their conversation now. He says, "Move it, people. I got a report of a limousine pulling into the Strand."

"Aleister!" breathes Livia. "He really is on his way here."

Julius climbs out of the empty water feature now, careful not to get his boots too muddy. The former swamp monster is close behind, muttering to himself about a trip to the Chinese laundry.

"Good to see you again, Yoshi," the old man shakes the boy's hand, looking genuinely pleased and relieved. "I'm delighted that you found what you were looking for, too," he adds, winking at Livia and the twins. "Encountering one psychic child is one thing. Meeting several in the space of a few days is either a miracle or fate. I prefer to think it's the latter, but let's discuss this back at the bunker. Under the circumstances, I think it might be safest if you all join Yoshi as our guests."

He turns to consult with his crew, only to jump aside on finding Billy so close behind.

"Yes, I know," says the Executive Deck Hand with a sigh. "I smell of ponds. It's hardly my fault, though."

"Never mind that now," says Julius. "Did we bring the rope?"

"Naturally." Billy touches two fingers to his lips and whistles sharply. A boy Yoshi recognises from the bunker hurries across with a tough-looking climbing rope looped over his shoulder. Billy takes it from him, asks everyone to stand at a safe distance, and focuses on the skylight above.

"What's the plan?" asks Yoshi, mystified, as Billy positions himself directly underneath it.

"I like to call it an escape strategy," he replies, without looking down. "The best gamers know how to get out of a situation before things get really messy." Billy pauses there, boggy water still dripping from his clothes, and considers what he's just said. "Now is not the time for details," he offers instead. "Give me some space to work here."

"Don't we need a grappling hook or something?" Yoshi looks up. The roof is one flat surface but for a skylight crammed with stars. As he sees it, there's no earthly means of anchoring the rope.

"Hurry," pleads the kid with the earpiece. "The limo is turning onto Threadneedle Street."

"Do it, Billy," says Mikhail. "Remember the magic words."

With an acid-tinged look at the kid with the red-spiked hair, Billy uncoils a loop of rope. "The only words I need to utter right now," he growls, "are 'back' and '*off*'!"

Yoshi does as instructed this time, ready to watch him swing the rope. Instead, Billy simply pushes one end through his fist. Instead of flopping as he continues to push, the rope rises as if pulled up on a string.

"That's a trick," declares Scarlett, like she's seen right through it.

"Of course it's a trick!" scoffs Billy. "The Indian Rope Trick is a classic of its kind. Only this time we don't plan to have one child climb to the top, but everyone who wants to leave. Now, please be quiet while I concentrate."

Yoshi turns to Julius, all out of amazement now. "What's wrong with the drain?" he asks. "Why can't we leave the way you arrived?"

Julius crinkles his nose. "Close encounter with

230

an alligator," he says, like it's some big secret, and promptly breaks away to encourage Billy in his bid to save them all.

27

WHAT GOES UP . . .

All eyes are on the rope. Inch by inch it rises towards the skylight. Finally the tip pokes through the gap that Yoshi had created. Billy coils the last of the length at his feet, and steps back proudly.

"*Voilà!*" he grins. "Who's going first? Not me this time, I can assure you all of that."

"I'll do it." One of the smaller kids grips the rope, and tugs it just to be sure. Quietly satisfied, he proceeds to shin up without any fear that it might collapse. Even before he's halfway up, Billy sends another crew member on their way.

Yoshi watches them go. He half suspects there must be some kind of wire inside, but doesn't care to find out now. What matters is that they're leaving, and with little time to spare. Julius stands beside him now, urging each climber to move quickly. "So what's going to happen once everyone is on the roof?" Yoshi asks, aware that he is the only free runner.

Julius smiles. "We thought perhaps you could teach us parkour. The crew caught sight of you on the cams. Some of them knew all about free running, but none of them were aware that you could do it. Now, all of them want to try it out."

"Even you?" asks Yoshi, not meaning to sound rude.

"Oh no." The old man chuckles at the thought. "This is as high as I've dared to come in decades. I think it was worth going the distance to save you, but it's time I headed back."

"You're going into the drain again?" Yoshi tips his head, confused. "What about the alligator?"

"The devil hasn't got me yet," says Julius, before turning to clamber back into the empty water feature. "Don't hang around," he warns the boy. "And bring as many special friends to the bunker as you can," he adds, gesturing at the highest floors. "Even thinking about taking to those stairs makes me feel giddy. Besides. I'd only hold you back."

"Will you be OK?" asks Yoshi, feeling a sudden wave of affection for this old man after all he's done for him. "Can you make it back on your own?"

Julius lowers his legs into the giant plughole. He looks down into it for a moment, and comes back smiling. "How can I get lost in my own world?" he asks.

"But what about the alligator?" Yoshi asks again.

Julius touches a finger to his lips, bidding the boy to keep that kind of talk to himself. "If we all believed there really is one lurking in the sewers," he says quietly, "every big-game hunter in the world would drop down to flush it out."

"But Julius—"

"Don't worry about me," he assures the boy with a wink. "There are a great many more dangers on the surface of the city than beneath it. I'll be just fine." And with that, Julius Grimaldi pushes himself off the lip of the drain. His straggly, snow-white hair and the tails of his coat seem to hang in the air momentarily, and then whip out of sight like he's just dropped into an abyss. With no time to check on him, Yoshi turns his attention to the balcony he's left behind.

"We have to get them out of here," he tells the girls at his side. By now, just Billy, Mikhail, and the kid with the earpiece remain at the foot of the rope. A column of determined-looking street urchins continues to clamber towards the skylight, where those who have already made it reach down to help.

Mikhail looks at Yoshi, sees him sizing up the stairs. At the same time, two fierce headlights sweep from one side of the lobby to the other, causing everyone to duck and turn around. Through the main glass doors, a white car can be seen pulling up in the forecourt.

"There's no time," says the Russian boy, gripping the rope for the kid with the earpiece now. *"Come on!"*

Yoshi faces the twins, ignoring his appeal. "That thing you do," he says. "Can you use it as a distraction?"

"You want fire?" asks Blaize, and sharpens one eyebrow. "Why didn't you ask earlier?"

With no time to stress the urgency of their situation, Yoshi turns to address the girl with the dark hair and dress. "Livia, I don't remember where the central lock is. You have to help!"

"Follow me," she says. "It's inside Aleister's office."

She dashes for a hallway behind them, not even glancing at the guard still sprawled on his back at the foot of the stairs. He's just coming round, and clearly seeing the wrong kind of stars. Yoshi hurries after her, ignoring Mikhail and Billy as they urge them to return, only for his thumping heart to sink on seeing his strange angel stop outside a door. She's frowning at a row of glowing digits on a panel beside the handle.

"It won't open!" he cries, trying the handle several times. "Everything is on lockdown!"

"It's Aleister who sets the code."

"Do you know it?" asks Yoshi hurriedly.

"I'm not a mind-reader," she reminds him, the haze of light around her like a torch in this dark recess. "What's frustrating is that there are several of them locked in their rooms up there."

"If they can pick up on my thoughts now," he mutters, "they'd know we tried our best."

Yoshi scans the numbers, not knowing where to start. It's a standard four-digit combination, but even he knows it could take a lot longer to crack than the minute or so they have left before the main man arrives. He toys with the nickel around his neck, counting out loud from one to four and back again. Livia enters both sequences in vain, and then punches the panel when nothing happens. She turns to Yoshi, despair in her eyes. Then her gaze falls to the dog tags around his neck. For he's stopped fretting with them now. Instead, Yoshi is pinching one of the plates so tightly he can feel the numbers imprinted on one side: *1, 1, 2* and *3*. He glances at Livia's own tag, finds she shares the same thing. Examining the other plate reveals her name followed by a *4*. Yoshi narrows his eyes, making more connections.

"There are others upstairs made to wear these tags," she tells him. "Nobody knows what this sequence is all about. The staff won't even say why we've each got another digit after our names. I'm worried my 4 shows the amount of years left before they let us go." She glances at the 5 after his name. "I always hoped I was wrong about that."

"How many have these tags?" asks Yoshi, punching in the number before she can speak.

"I can't be sure," she admits. "Six of us, maybe. Seven, counting you."

Yoshi stabs the *enter* button as she says this. The numbers turn from red to green, as does Livia's aura.

Yoshi stays on the threshold of this, the main office, keeping watch on both sides. The office is sparse. Just a big oak desk with a half-smoked cigar in an ashtray. A high-backed leather swivel chair is behind it, facing the wrong way. Yoshi can almost see the brute sitting there. Just a glimpse of his bald crown, before he spins around and scares the living daylights out of some poor kid caught up in all of this. The faint crunch of footsteps on gravel reminds him exactly where the very man is right now: outside the building, but on his way in.

"Hurry," he hisses into the office. "As fast as you can!"

Livia heads directly for another panel of buttons on the far wall. She's been here before, or at least scoped it out on a previous visit. Deftly, she selects two buttons. The first triggers an almighty clapping sound. The locks withdrawing, Yoshi hopes and

237

prays. The second causes a click and then a hiss of static when Livia breathes into a microphone spot underneath it.

"*The doors are open,*" she announces, and immediately her voice booms around the building. "*All the guards have gone. You still have time before Aleister arrives, so run for the hills, my friends! Go home to your families and leave this place behind!*"

"What about Aleister?" Yoshi holds out for an answer, but already Livia has finished her broadcast and is dashing for the door.

"The element of surprise is on our side right now," she calls back to him. "Your magician mates just showed me that."

28

LEAP OF FAITH

It could be an avalanche, such is the noise that greets the pair as they sprint for the lobby. The first kids to thunder down the stairs reach the marble floor just before Yoshi. They fan out for the main doors, spilling around the weed-matted basin that was once a water feature, cheering and hooting wildly. High above, framing the skylight, he sees his crew hauling Billy and then Mikhail onto the roof. They're yelling at the twins to climb the rope, but Blaize and Scarlett keep their eyes fixed on the lobby doors, true to the boy who is savouring every last detail of this moment.

Yoshi spins around gleefully, sees Livia watching the scene unfold. Washes of bright colour shimmer and swoop around her, and then change quite dramatically. Her eyes clearly meet something coming through the doors, and those psychic fireworks freeze and turn ice-blue.

"Oh dear," says Yoshi, registering the change. "We're too late, aren't we?"

She nods, not even blinking. The boy turns. He sees the last few kids run wide for the doors, then scramble to clear this looming figure who has just stepped inside. There he is, with moonshine behind him, the bald brute in the mink coat. This man he now knows as Aleister calmly removes one leather glove after the other. Yoshi meets those tight blue eyes, his own fear matched by fury and frustration at not making it out in time. Slowly, the whoops and cries from the escaping kids fade. Instead, a silence fills the space on the back of all the cold air coming in through the open door. Even the crew on the roof pull back from the skylight, as if they can't bear to witness the fate of the boy and his friends.

"Welcome home, Yoshi. All that time searching the streets, and I find you've returned to the fold voluntarily."

As soon as Aleister speaks, Yoshi recognises his voice. It doesn't quite match his body, he remembers, thinking back to their last exchange as he cowered from the man under a buckled vent. There's no boom or bass to carry it. Instead it seems to float and weave through the air. A strange-sounding hiss, almost, with a hint of the orient in his accent.

"I'm not planning on staying," replies Yoshi,

squaring his shoulders now. "I only popped in to catch up with friends."

"And let them loose like *this*?" Aleister spits back suddenly. He glares across the lobby, only to his restore his calm just as abruptly. "Then again, I suppose among the scores of children you have just ejected, only a handful showed real promise." He pauses there, acknowledging Livia and the twins with a nod. "In fact, it appears you've made a fine selection yourself. All four of you have proven your potential, after all. You should wear your tags with pride!" Yoshi sees Blaize and Scarlett pick at little plates around their necks. He doesn't need to inspect them to feel sure that he and Livia share the same sequence of numbers as the twins.

"What do you want with us?" asks Livia, stepping up beside Yoshi now. "Our families signed us over because we need help to understand ourselves. We need to know why we're different, and how we can control our gifts. All you've done is drag us around churches and make us feel like we're letting you down!"

Aleister spreads his big hands. "With three more specimens like you, believe me, I'd be thrilled by your abilities."

"*Seven*," breathes Yoshi, working things through in his mind. "Seven psychics, for seven ley lines in the ring."

The sound of slow clapping draws his attention back across the lobby.

"Well done," growls Aleister. "It seems your little field trip has taught you a great deal. It's a shame you've set my project back by months, but I can always find more children who share your gift. Now, go to your rooms before I have to show you the kind of power that I hope one day you'll demonstrate for me."

"No way," spits Yoshi, and marches to the point on the floor directly under the skylight. "This show is over, Aleister. We're out of here." He reaches for the rope, ready to anchor it for Livia and the twins. Just as soon as he grips it, however, the whole thing collapses onto the floor. The boy looks in shock at the tangle, and then peers up sharply. A head pops over the edge of the skylight. It's Billy, looking sheepish.

"Didn't anyone teach you the trick?" Billy calls down, and then snaps angrily over his shoulder: "Who was supposed to instruct Yoshi? It was on the memo that went round when he arrived . . . what? It was supposed to be *me*? Are you sure? Oh!"

"Billy, just get us out of here!" cries Yoshi, aware that the brute has begun to advance across the floor. "Help us!"

"There's only one trick you can pull now!" Billy

calls down, cupping his hands so the boy can hear him. "The vanishing act!"

"Where are the mirrors?" yells Yoshi, as the twins step together to block the brute's path.

"You don't need any!" shouts Billy. "You just need to run as fast as you can!"

"Oh thanks!" Abandoning all hope of escaping via the roof, Yoshi wheels around, searching for an exit. Aleister is closing in now, ruling out any dash for the doors. He sees the twins step in front of his path and join hands tightly. A second later, the ground beneath the brute's feet begins to smoulder. Aleister looks down, smiles to himself as if in approval, and continues to advance, unconcerned. With Livia at his side, Yoshi watches this fiery defence cooling rapidly. Briefly, he considers throwing the rope into the drain down which Julius dropped, but there's just no time now. All he can do is grab Livia by the wrist, yell, "Follow me!" and scramble over the rocks into the silted swamp bed.

"Where are we going?" She splashes after him, across the matted bed of weeds, and then digs in her heels when he stops at the black hole in the middle. "Are you crazy?"

It had alarmed the boy to see Julius appear to freefall into this drain, but what choice does he have? "This way!" he calls to the twins, as they retreat over the rocks on the other side, and join them on the swamp floor.

"What's down there?" asks Scarlett.

"We're about to find out." Yoshi glances at the brute now hauling himself over the rocks towards them. "All I know is our only chance now is to go underground."

"You're the boss," says Blaize, coming up behind the boy now as if she might protect him. "Just don't you dare suggest 'ladies first'," she finishes, and without warning gives Yoshi a hefty shove. "If this is a leap of faith, we're following *you!*"

29

WHERE DOES IT END?

It's a hole into hell! This is the first thing Yoshi thinks on plunging into the gloom. Being pushed in was the first surprise, just as it is to drop past the overflow gully that the crew must have crawled through to get here. Finding nothing underneath him now is the real shocker, and for a second or so the freefall is more like an out of body experience. He can see himself plunging into darkness, arms flailing to keep himself upright. Fleetingly, something brushes his backside. He feels it again, but this time it seems to scoop him forwards. The third time he connects with this steep, smooth surface, Yoshi whoops out loud. The chute they're in might be inclined like a mountain slope, but it's levelling out now and delivering him from danger at full tilt. He glances up behind him, spots three dots within a shrinking circle of light.

"Enjoy the ride!" he yells, half laughing as the

velocity pulls his stomach into shapes. "We're safe now—"

The splash takes his breath away. Yoshi cuts off his own sentence with a gasp, and then quickly finds his feet. In this gloom he can barely see his own hands. What he senses clearly enough is that he's chest deep in something wet that doesn't smell quite right. Behind him in the chute, the glow from Livia's aura begins to brighten. As it casts a light on the watery surface, Yoshi figures all will become clear soon enough, only to find out, face first, when the girl herself torpedoes in behind him. It isn't quite sewage, but then neither is it goat's milk. This is the run-off from London's gutters, with the exception of the odd sneaky addition, plumbed in on the sly like so much of the city's waterworks.

"Yuk!" she splutters, attempting to keep her hands from the stagnant drain-water. The twins crash in next, one after the other, which puts paid to Livia's bid to stay clean. Then Yoshi surfaces, coughing and spluttering, and the three girls count themselves lucky.

"Well," says Livia acidly. "That went well." Her aura hangs high over her, as if unwilling to touch the surface of this swill. Even so, the misty light is enough for everyone to see that they've splashed into a narrow, brickwork channel. For a second, all four turn in the soup, and then a heavy sliding sound washes in from the mouth of the drain.

"He's coming," gasps Scarlett. "He's actually coming down after us!"

"Another good reason to move on," her sister adds, grimacing at the smell rising into their nostrils.

"This way!" shouts Yoshi. "Follow the current."

It's tough to wade at speed. Even so, this small band have good reason not to complain. Behind them, the mouth of the drain begins to groan under the weight of the incoming body.

"Let me go first," insists Livia. "At least we can see where we're heading."

Yoshi moves to one side, glancing back as he does so. At the same time, the rushing noise cuts to silence, followed immediately by what sounds like a depth charge going off back there.

"We have company," he mutters, and pushes on behind Livia and the twins.

With the aura illuminating the way ahead, it's hard to see what's happening under the mouth of the drain. The light behind them weakens with every step they take, and shadows begin to move in. Yoshi doesn't like it one bit – the way this fog of darkness seems to merge over the water and reach out towards them.

"Look, up ahead!" This is Scarlett, pointing now. Yoshi turns to see what appears to be a sudden end to the channel. The gutter water just melts into the bed. At first it looks as if the high bank of silt behind it serves as some kind of dam. Coming closer, into the shallows, it becomes clear the flow is draining through yet another grille.

"Just how far down does this city go?" mutters Blaize, picking up her pace now, like everyone else. "Where does it end?"

"Unless we move faster," pants Yoshi, turning one more time to see a black cloak filling the tunnel, "it ends right here for us all."

Livia is first to leap the drain, her shoes sinking into the silt bank on the other side. Blaize follows with a look of grim determination, while both her sister and Yoshi pull a face when their bare feet meet what feels like cold porridge.

"*Yeeeew!*" complains Scarlett, but pushes on all the same.

Scrambling up beside her now, Yoshi wonders why the others have stopped dead. He takes one look at the river crossing their path, and punches the air.

"*Yeeees!*"

Resting her hands on her knees to catch her breath, Livia looks up at him and frowns. "We're in the guts of the city. We're wet, chilled to the bone and on the run. What's to celebrate?"

The steady sloshing sound way back in the channel creates a sense of urgency in the situation.

With no time to explain himself, Yoshi simply points out two deep tracks of footprints running beside the river.

"I know where we are," he tells them, scanning the tracks to get his bearings. "We need to go this way!"

"How can you be sure?" asks Scarlett.

Somewhere downriver just then, close enough for all of them to hear it, something big and reptile-like makes its presence known. It's the soft splash, and then the swishing noise through water that causes them all to catch their breath.

Blaize turns around smartly. "Did I just hear an alligator? There's no such thing as an alligator in the sewers, is there? It's an urban myth."

Yoshi is more concerned that the sloshing behind the silt bank has turned to splashing footfalls. "This way," he pleads with them, itching to keep moving now. "If Aleister wants to bring out the best in us, I know the very place that we can put on a surprise show for him."

An old sheet of newspaper lies on the empty platform. The headlines report on another Blitz bombing raid. The picture shows London's skyline ablaze, with searchlights reaching for the sky. The dome of St Paul's can be seen in the middle distance. It's unscathed and seemingly afloat upon a sea of smoke and flames. The paper stirs all of a sudden, and lifts into the air. When the train slams out from the tunnel and speeds through the ghost station, this old sheet loops gracefully, and then glides to rest once more. Time and again it has carried out this little display, but there's never anyone here to witness it. Until now. Except on this occasion the boy who leads the way up the footbridge is more concerned about staging a display of his own.

"What *is* this place?" Livia stops to catch her breath. "It isn't on the tube map, is it?"

"Not any more," says the boy, surveying the length of this ghost station once again. Reaching up on tiptoe next, Yoshi brushes at the brick overhead with the seven-pointed star etched into it. Soot comes off on his fingers. He comes back down, makes sure the girls are watching, and rubs his hands together.

"Hey!" cries Scarlett as the black dust that falls away appears to transform into sparkling atoms. "How did you do that?"

"Try it out yourself," Yoshi suggests, keeping one eye on the foot tunnel that just led them to this forgotten underground station. He steps back to let the girls give it a shot, but doesn't share their sense of awe and wonder at the miraculous results.

For a shadow is spilling from the foot tunnel now, like ink from an unseen source.

Scarlett eyes the black mass nervously. "If we're going to catch a train out of here," she says to Yoshi, "shouldn't we be on the platform?"

"Don't even think about asking me to jump onto the roof and surf out of here," Blaize tells him. "If I'm going to die I'd sooner do it with some dignity."

"We're not going to die," says Livia. "Are we?"

Yoshi finds it hard to look her in the eyes. "There's a church above us," he says, drawing their attention upwards. "One of seven."

The twins groan together. "Now you're sounding like Aleister," says Blaize. "Spare us the lecture. Just tell us what to do."

The boy opens his mouth to explain about waypoints and ley lines, but Livia gasps and points along the platform. At the far end, they catch the shadow snake out onto the tracks, and there adopt both substance and shape. Black turns to white in a blink, and the bald brute in the mink who faces up to them grins like he's heard every word.

"Go ahead and show them, little boy," he hisses. "Seeing is believing, after all."

Yoshi scowls, curling his fingers in and out of fists. Then, with his eyes fixed on the figure encircled by the tunnel's dark mouth, he reaches for the stone and braces himself for the torrent of water. He tries to picture the other end of the ley line, another star shape in a stone under a stream, and relief flows over him as the sound of a deluge builds.

"Brace yourselves," he tells the girls. "This is going to be big."

30

HERE WE GO

Aleister folds his arms high across his chest. He looks totally unconcerned, even when Yoshi gives him one final warning. It's only when the rushing water soars in volume and clarity that the brute turns to face the tunnel, and calmly snaps two fingers together.

Immediately, the noise tapers to a trickle. Instead of crashing white rapids a splash of water slaps between the tracks, and fizzes into the ballast bed. The boy is stunned. It's as if someone had simply chucked a bucketful out from the blackness and switched off the sound effects.

"Now *that*," says Aleister, stepping back to face them squarely, "is magick."

"You stopped it!" cries Yoshi, as enraged as he is embarrassed.

"Maybe it's just not the waypoint for you," suggests Aleister, still playing with him. "Waypoint

253

number five has your name all over it. Just like it says on your tag."

"*Yoshi 5*," the boy mutters to himself, without even touching the nickel plate that had baffled Billy when he first dropped into the bunker. "So that explains it."

"This waypoint is number three," continues Aleister. "It was destined for one of the kids you turned on to the streets. You might be able to tap into a little energy from here, but a touch from the right key master would've caused havoc. Bummer, huh?"

Yoshi slams his palm on the stone one more time, but nothing happens. Sensing his helplessness, Aleister moves towards them. The amusement on his face is over, instantly. Now, his blue eyes harden, and the crease across his brow sinks sharply in the middle.

"Let me try!" Livia reaches for the stone, straining to touch it with her fingertips. On contact, her aura seems to concentrate around her, and travel up her arm. The closer it gets to the stone, the brighter it grows, as if something is about to blow. Yoshi steps back, as do the twins. Even Aleister stops on the track, forced now to shield his eyes as if staring into the sun . . .

"This may not be my number either!" she screams, upon which a molten ball of energy shoots at the figure on the tracks. "But I'm mad as hell with you!" The impact knocks the brute off his feet, carries him the length of the platform, and vanishes on smashing him into the track.

Livia dusts her hands, ignoring the look of sheer amazement fixed on the faces of her friends. At the tunnel mouth, Aleister stirs and tests his limbs. He coughs and groans as he picks himself up, and then shakes his head as if trying to clear his vision. "You're stronger than I thought," he informs the girl, and straightens himself out to his full height. "With my help," he adds, glowering at them once again, "you could use the fire inside you all to grow stronger still."

Yoshi turns to the twins. He doesn't need to tell them what to do. They don't even consult each other, just reach up as one and connect with the stone.

"Even if this ain't our stone either," Scarlett tells him, "you're still faced with double trouble!"

With a sound like a sheet snapping open, two tongues of fire race out of the tunnel, setting the rails ablaze. The flames overtake Aleister, who stops and admires what they've done. Yoshi watches from the handrail, despairing at what he sees. By rights Aleister should be fleeing for his life, but not even this heat looks like it can touch him.

"My word, you're *all* growing strong," he tells

them, with both paws clasped behind his back. "Just think of the fun we could have had with *seven* of us. With each of us tuned into a waypoint in the ring, this city could have been our playground."

"That's never going to happen!" yells Yoshi, and reaches for the stone the twins are still touching. Livia follows his lead, her aura encircling their hands. On the tracks, the flames rise up with a roar. Yoshi glances down, feeling the heat on the soles of his feet, and jumping back when it becomes too hot to handle. From the mouth of the tunnel, Aleister locks his gaze onto them, and once more begins to walk towards them.

"Just look what you can do when you put your minds together," he tells them. "We really could be an unbeatable force. If you can't open your eyes to the possibilities, I'll just have to open them for you."

As he speaks, Yoshi feels a wisp of air meet his face. He blinks in response, still watching the brute move towards them. The breeze picks up swiftly, disturbing a newspaper sheet on the platform. And then, way down the tunnel, two spots of light begin to grow. Yoshi focuses on the man once again, sees his shadow stretch slowly ahead of him as the lights in the tunnel grow bigger and brighter. *A train ... A train is coming.* He whispers the words to himself, torn now by the predicament he's facing. For a second he considers saying nothing, but it's no good. He can't stand by and watch this happen.

"Aleister," he calls out. "Get off the line!"

"Nice try." He curls his fat fingers like claws, hissing *"It's behind you!"*, as if that's what the boy should've said instead. "If this is your idea of a distraction technique," he continues, oblivious to the way the flames begin to flicker and lick with the wind, "you really should try harder."

"It isn't going to stop!" cries Livia.

"That's enough!" Aleister looks furious with them now, still blinkered to the fact that it isn't just flames that are roaring down the tracks. "Now shut up," he thunders, "and watch what I have to show you. What you're about to see might seem incredible, unearthly, even *diabolical*—"

"No!" Yoshi screams from the bridge one final time, but even he knows it's too late now. As the headlamps knife out of the blackness, the brute finally registers the horror barrelling towards him. He wheels around, twisting into his own shadow, it seems to the boy, who reels away with his eyes squeezed tight shut. The train thunders under the footbridge, rattling every nut and bolt. With his back turned, Yoshi dares to open his eyes, and watches the last carriage shrink into a dark, consuming gloom. It seems to blacken beyond shadow, he thinks, but senses somehow that nothing will come out of it to surprise them this time.

"He's gone." This is Livia, the first on her feet. She waits for Yoshi and the twins to collect themselves, and nods to the place where Aleister had been standing.

The tracks are no longer ablaze. They're blackened and smoking, a sure sign they hadn't imagined it, but the man in the mink is nowhere to be seen.

"But is he gone for good?" asks Yoshi, thinking that a true magician would have made the most of that crucial final moment when his audience could bear to look no longer.

"Right now," sighs Blaize, "I don't care if he's dead or alive. All I want to do is freshen up, grab a smoothie to go, and lie down some place quiet."

"She means it," warns Scarlett. "If we don't get going we'll all feel the heat."

Yoshi smiles, and then laughs when Blaize pulls a face at her sister. It feels good, enjoying a moment with friends. He might not recall all the times they've shared together in the past, but this is one he'll never forget.

"Do you know how to get us out of here?" asks Livia, stepping up close as if to read his response.

"Sure I do," he says, wondering if he really can find his way back to the bunker from here. All he can be certain about is the fact that there must be a thousand and one ways to get around the city without once coming up for fresh air.

"Guys!" This is Blaize. The note of alarm in her voice causes them all to face her, and then follow her line of sight to the shadow emerging from the foot tunnel.

"Oh no," breathes Livia. "Here we go again."

Yoshi steps in front of them all, prepared to do whatever it takes to protect his soul mates, and then promptly stands down with a private smile. "This is no threat," he tells them, as an elderly figure shuffles out onto the platform, and stoops to inspect the headlines on the newspaper at his feet. "It's our guide home!"

Julius Grimaldi looks up on hearing Yoshi's voice. "Did I miss the performance?" he asks. "Oh well, I'm sure there'll be another chance to see it some time."

"Maybe so," says Yoshi, leaning against the rail with the others.

The old man nods to himself, both eyes sparkling now. "Would your guests care to join us in the bunker?" he asks. "You look a little washed-out up there."

Yoshi glances at Livia's aura. The haze is certainly weaker than before, which is no surprise after what they've been through. He thinks about his own gift, and wonders if there'll ever come a time when he can summon it at will just like the twins. "Let's go," he says, turning now to leave the bridge.

"I'm hoping the crew will be home by the time we get there," says Julius, greeting them each in turn on the platform. Yoshi stands last in line, his memory intact but his mind elsewhere when the old man clasps his hand. "Even the galley was deserted when I popped in just now. I'm hoping that means they've stopped off on the way home to pick up some sushi . . ." Julius pauses there, wondering why the boy has not responded, and then smiles when he sees that flash go off inside his eyes. "What do you see?" he asks, abandoning what he'd planned to share with them about his passion for raw fish and rice.

Yoshi smiles, his focus slack. "I see a lot of young punks on a rooftop under the stars. It looks like they've been there a while. Like they're stuck or something. Some are playing cards. Others are lying back checking out the constellations."

"My kind of people," murmurs Julius.

"Seems they might be waiting for something or someone," Yoshi continues, and then blinks as if he's just been struck by an urgent thought.

He turns to the Livia and the twins, clearly with them again. "I'll catch you later," he says, retreating from them now. "I really have to be some place."

"Be careful!" warns Julius, as if he knows full well that Yoshi is about to take to the city's upper levels.

Livia switches her attention from the old man to the boy. Yoshi is beginning to look pained, like this just can't wait. "Where are you going?" she asks. "What's the hurry?"

"There are some street magicians I'd like you to meet," says Yoshi finally, and spreads his hands like there'll be another time to share the whole story, "but first I need to teach them a few tricks from *my* book!"

ABOUT THE AUTHOR

Matt Whyman is the author of *Boy Kills Man*, *The Wild* and *Superhuman*, as well as the non fiction advice books for boys, *XY* and *XY2*. He is an agony uncle for AOL and Bliss magazine, and part of the award-winning team at The Site, the UK's leading online info resource for young people. *Key to the City* is the first title in the So Below sequence. You can visit Matt on his website at www.mattwhyman.com

SIEGE UNDER THE CITY

It's 1666, and London is ablaze. Below ground, a band of desperate citizens seek refuge from The Great Fire, only to be buried alive when the buildings collapse into the tunnels.

According to the story, these poor souls survived.

Now, centuries later, it is said that their descendants still exist in the very bowels of the city. Blind from a life without sunshine, but with senses as sharp as their teeth, this savage tribe are to be avoided at all costs. Which isn't so easy when Julius concludes the final waypoint in the Faerie Ring is located in their lair…

With the fate of the city in his hands, can Yoshi infiltrate this forbidden domain and escape with his life?

So Below 2 - Siege Under the City. ISBN: 1-416-90097-7

Twice the magic. Double the mayhem.
Surfacing soon in a bookshop near you.

TO BE A NINJA BY BENEDICT JACKA

Ignis and Allandra are on the run. Escaping from the clutches of their drug baron father, they have managed to find sanctuary deep in the forest, while Allandra's twin, Michael, has been re-captured. Their new home: Rokkaku, a secret training school for ninjas.

For the rebellious Ignis, stumbling upon the hidden school is the last thing he wants – replacing one set of rules and regulations with another. For Allandra, it offers the perfect hiding place, and a chance to make true friends at last. But each day is a struggle: avoiding discovery, bowing to rules, dealing with bullies and going through rigorous training. Finally Allandra sets off to rescue her twin – but can she save Michael, without sacrificing herself?

ISBN: 1-416-90128-0

HURRICANE FORCE BY MALCOLM ROSE

What would happen if we could use the weather as a weapon?

Jake's father died in mysterious circumstances – now Jake, who shares a similar skill for predicting the weather, takes on his mantle. But can he prevent his father's research falling into the wrong hands, and stop the US military from using it for nefarious means?

Award-winning author and research scientist, Malcolm Rose, turns his formidable talent to warfare, and the weather.

ISBN: 0-689-87284-4